Courage comes in many forms.

From trusting the unbelievable,

To your heroes surprising you,

To protecting your best friend,

To pursuing the clues no matter where they lead,

To, yes, saving an innocent life.

*For everyone who's ever gone through with it
Even when they were afraid.*

CAPELESS HEROES

TALES OF EVERYDAY SAVIORS

JASON A. ADAMS

SPIRAL PUBLISHING, LTD.

CONTENTS

INTRODUCTION

Heeeere they come to save the day!

Who doesn't love a good hero or heroine? A dashing crusader swooping in to defeat the villain's dastardly plan. The masked man cleaning up the town before riding off into the sunset. The mysterious stranger who arrives in the nick of time to unravel the wicked wizard's evil enchantment.

I love those stories, too. But even more, I love stories about ordinary people, whose tiny acts of heroism never make the news.

From parents raising their kids right, to people getting turtles out of the road, to folks doing something that scares them to death, just because it needs to be done.

This type of hero is all around us. And more often that we might think, inside us as well. Think of the adults who said just the right thing when you were young, some nugget of wise advice that you've never forgotten. Think of the guy who knew just what to do when your car wouldn't start, or the librarian who found the perfect book to help you through a trying time.

Who are these people, if not heroes?

The stories in this collection explore those everyday heroes and heroines. From a state trooper who has to rescue her partner in a very un-policelike way, to a young man trying to decide what to do with his life. From a teenage girl trying to help her best friend, to a puppy's savior.

I couldn't resist slipping in a true knight of the streets. Dirk Knight, that is. My favorite aspiring private eye, who always manages to save the day in spite of himself. Poor guy, he still doesn't get to be the closer.

So come on a ride-along with this band of unlikely saviors. See if you recognize them in those you meet next time you go to the grocery store.

Who knows? You might be someone's hero, and you never even realized.

You'll find more stories with Dirk, Trooper Foyle, and the young hero of "Freeing the Spirit" at www. jasonadams.info. While you're there, sign up for regular updates from the Brain Squirrels about upcoming stories, travel news, pictures of the cats who rescued me, and whatever else strikes my fancy come newsletter time.

Happy heroing!

JASON A. ADAMS
Author of To Catch a Thief
If You're There

For everyone who trusts a good dog's nose.

Chapter 1

God, if you're there, please cast the inventor of departmental audits into the deepest, hottest lake of napalm you've got.

Joan Foyle sighed and opened yet another folder full of hoary old paperwork that stank of mildew and rodent turds.

The semi-decennial audit would be the death of her, and had her seriously considering dipping into the evidence room's stash.

The Wise County office of the Virginia State Police's drug enforcement division wasn't the busiest in the Commonwealth, by any means. But that meant that the regular, irregular sieving of old reports and collation of case files didn't happen near often enough.

And she'd only been working for the DED for less than two years, so this was her first rodeo.

As low woman on the totem, she drew the lucky straw and had spent the last two days going through all the files in the office's fifteen cabinets, checking to see if all the Ts were dotted and the Is crossed.

Her own eyes were definitely crossed after half a ton of paperwork. In triplicate.

She grabbed another folder, this one labeled *Analysis of Items Recovered from Lick Fork Mine Shaft #3*. That had been a good one.

She hadn't been involved in that raid. She'd read about it in the newspaper, back before she had a valid driver's license. A bunch of bootleggers had decided herbal products would be more profitable than booze, and had filled an abandoned coal shaft with grow lights and wooden tubs full of imported mary jane.

No one had caught on to the operation until the crew managed to blow the transformer they were stealing power from.

Joan added the folder to the obsolete pile, wincing at the sting in her fingertips. The ancient, mummified paper was sucking every last bit of moisture from her hands. And she couldn't slather on some lotion, for fear of staining the oh-so-important fossil record.

She picked up her coffee mug. Took a cautious sip, and pulled a face she could feel all the way down to her knees. Cop coffee had a well-deserved reputation already, and this particular example of the dark arts had gone as cold and bitter as Ms. Haversham in that old Dickens novel.

Joan stood up, admiring the display her body's percussion section gave as various under-worked joints tried to get used to their first new position in hours. Time to give the audit a rest and go for a quick walk around the parking lot.

The commander couldn't knock her for trying to keep herself in peak physical condition, right?

Outside, she squinted against the sunbeams that cut down from the ridge to the west, skewering her overworked eyes. She welcomed the light, though. At least it wasn't fluorescent.

As the sun's warmth fought against late April's cool breeze, Joan went through a quick set of limbering up exercises. She'd been out of school for more years than she cared to admit, but she still used her old softball and track routines to keep the ol' muscles loose and (hopefully) toned.

Hell. Maybe something would happen to take her away from that damn desk and those double-damned stacks of folders.

Joan was on her third lap around the parking lot, wondering if she should tell Trooper Hines that his left rear tire needed some air, when Jace Everett began singing about the bad things he wanted to do with her.

Larry. Her big, handsome sheriff of a boyfriend.

Boyfriend. She still couldn't get used to that word, even after two years. She hadn't had a *boyfriend* since college. And never one that lit her match the way Larry did. He'd been her boss at one time, until she gave up her deputy's star to take the job with the state police. A good career move, and a better personal one, since there weren't any rules about cops in different agencies dating, now were there?

She felt the smile that she couldn't do a thing about as she pulled her phone from her belt and hit the magic button.

"Hey there, sugarbear. Are you calling to tell me I've been recalled to county service and won't be able to finish my paperwork, more's the pity?"

A laugh came through the phone. One that warmed her in all the right places.

"Sorry, sugarplum. About all I can do for you is a

bucket of chicken from Lulu's, and a reserved spot on the sofa."

She sighed again. With pleasure and anticipation this time.

"Sounds heavenly. Want me to meet you there, or do you need to come here and arrest me?"

And there was that laugh again.

"There might be handcuffs in your future, young lady. But not until you finish every bite of the fudge cake a certain extremely generous lawman baked up this afternoon. If you can get away in the next few minutes, it might even still be warm when you get here."

Joan checked her watch. 5:30. Past her usual quitting time. Screw the audit!

"Sheriff, I shall keep my bubble flashing and my wailer wailing as I abuse every speed limit between here and that cake."

Chapter 2

THERE'S nothing like a good breakfast after a night of good sex and good sleep, both with the man you love more than life. More than fudge cake, even. If that's possible.

Joan sat at Larry's kitchen table, enjoying the cool air against her flesh. He still hadn't got used to the fact that she wore clothes all day, and saw no reason to wear them when she didn't need to.

"Any visitors last night?" she said, taking a drink of good not-cop coffee while she could.

"Nope, not last night. Why? You expectin' trouble?"

Larry had told her about how his long-dead great-grandmother came in his dreams, sometimes. When there was something he needed to know, or something he needed special help with. She didn't want to believe in ghosts, what her own grandmother called *haints*, but she'd experienced a bit too much weirdness since cuffing herself to his wrist to rule anything out.

He puttered around between fridge, stove, and table, setting a plate full of grits and eggs in front of her. She couldn't help but check that fine backside of his. He might have a little bit of snow on his rooftop, but Larry Crabtree was still a fine-looking hunk of lawman.

And he looked cute as anything with his Granny's old flowery apron on over his brown sheriff's uniform.

"So what's on your agenda today, my good sheriff?" she said between bites of the best eggs she'd ever tasted. What all did he put in them, anyway?

"Ah, I got to get on out to Floyd Davis' place," he said, sitting down with his own food. "We got a call about how Floyd's boy Gary is driving around in a brand-new Dodge Charger, and the whole family on assistance."

She took another bite, this time with a chaser of steaming cheese grits that had her sucking air.

"Gary Davis. Nephew of Archie Davis. Hmm."

Larry gave her a look.

"What's that *hmm* about, Joanie? You know something I should?"

She shrugged, wiped a smear of grits from her right breast. That was gonna leave a red spot.

"Well, I know Archie was once upon a time part of a ring of moonshiners and dope runners. He was one of the ones busted when that mine shaft got raided back in the early Nineties."

Larry laughed and had to wipe bits of egg off his chin.

"Oh, yeah. The Great Dickenson County Pot Mine. Did you know that all eight folks arrested turned state's evidence? And that nary a one of them went to jail? I'd still like to know whose bank account was behind that little shindig."

Joan laughed along with him. Small town goings-on

never ceased to amaze her, and she'd grown up here. At least *her* county hadn't ever been raided by the feds for a political bribery scheme involving prize 'coon hounds like that place up by the West Virginia line.

"Anyway," she said, using her fork to scrape up every last speck of Larry's delicious cooking. "Watch out if you go up there. Floyd's a character, but he's harmless. Who knows what all whoever's involved with Gary might be up to, though?"

"Ten-four, Trooper Foyle," he said, taking the trashbag full of last night's leftovers and chicken buckets from the can and knotting the top. "You want me to call you directly if I find anything? Or do I need to go through channels, so folks won't think we're up to hanky-panky?"

"That depends," she said, standing and stretching until her back crackled. The way his eyes lit up was probably the best compliment she'd get all day. "Show me what sort of hanky-panky you're talking about, big boy."

Chapter 3

Finally!

At three-thirty, Joan closed the last folder, and put it on the last pile. Three days and umpteen thousand sheets of paper, but she'd finally gotten through the last moldy oldie in the filing cabinets. Surely she deserved a promotion and a raise.

"Bout time you finished up," came a gruff voice. "We were wondering if you'd been sleeping on the job."

Lt. Harris. Her boss, and usually an all-right guy. Six-two and built like someone who spends most of his free time in the gym, Harris turned every whiskerless head in three counties. Pity he preferred whiskered heads. Not that Joan herself ever noticed his tight bod or anything.

"You know what?" she said, threatening him with her stapler. A trained person could do a *lot* with a stapler. "I think I'm just gonna quit. Like right now."

He laughed, and set a cup of coffee with a famous

name on the side in front of her. She inhaled as deep as she could. That was definitely *not* cop coffee.

"Won't work," she said through a mouthful of drool. "I'm incorruptible and can't be bought."

"How about a short-term lease, then?"

He set a glazed donut down beside the coffee, still hot and gooey from the fryer.

"Okay, you win," she said, snatching the donut before he changed his mind. "I'll stay. On a provisional basis."

"Can't tell you how much I appreciate all the hard work, Foyle," Harris said, sitting on the corner of her desk. "I had to do that hell my first year here. Not something I'd wish on my worst enemy."

"I can't say it's been fun, but—"

The cartoonish strain of *I'm Forever Blowing Bubbles* came from her desk. Joan groaned, and picked up the phone.

"Hey, Pauline. What's up?"

Pauline was the dispatcher/receptionist/secretary combo at the Dickenson County Sheriff's Office. Larry groused about her annoying habits, like the incessant gum chewing. And popping. But she was a decent kid. Just turned twenty-three, and already had Cal, Larry's deputy, wrapped around her purple-nailed finger.

"Hey, Joanie. Have you heard from Larry? He hasn't checked in for over four hours."

Pauline's normally cheerful-to-the-point-of-nauseating voice sounded tense. Worried.

Joan's shoulder blades tried to join up and punch her in the back of the head.

"When's the last time you heard from him, Pauline? Where was he? Have you checked the bug on his prowler?"

All county and state vehicles were equipped with GPS locators. Not always good for much in the coalfields, with their long ridges and narrow valleys, but she should at least have a last-known on the tracker.

"Yeah. First thing when I noticed the time. His patrol car is at his place. Hasn't moved since this morning. But he called in before he headed out to the Davis place, and that was after the last timestamp on the GPS."

Almost two minutes, and not one gum pop. Anything that got Pauline to stop chewing her cud...

Holding up a finger to Harris as she quickly scooped up her purse and checked her keys, Joan tried to think. If Larry had gone up to the Davis place, why was his prowler sitting at home?

"Listen, Pauline. You stay put, you hear? Don't you *dare* leave that desk until one of us talks to Sheriff Crabtree. Where's Deputy Fleming?"

"He... Uh, I think he went up Sandy Ridge Road. Toward the Davis place. With all the guardrail work going on up there, he thought maybe...that Larry..." Now her young voice had gone thick and hiccupy.

Joan felt that way herself, but it wouldn't do anyone a damn bit of good.

"That's good, Pauline. Real good. Get Cal on the squawkbox, tell him *not* to stop at Floyd Davis' place. Tell him he can drive by, check the driveway, but no knocking on the door until we get some cavalry arranged. Just in case. I'm going to check at Larry's house. Just in case."

In case of what, she didn't know. The Davis' were rumrunning scoundrels, but Floyd was about as dangerous as a twinkie in a rain barrel.

"I'll call you from there. *You* best buzz *me* the split second you hear from Larry, got me?"

If she heard from Larry.

God, if you're there, keep my man above the daisies.

"What's up, Joan?" Lt. Harris put his hand on her arm. Gently. And she managed to not shove him out the window. "Need me to call a patrol trooper?"

"Not yet," she said on her way out. "But stand by, okay? And thanks for the donut, sir."

Chapter 4

Joan drove like a trucker on speed and a tight dead-line, sliding across the gravels in front of the old Crab-tree homeplace where she'd spent so many happy days and nights barely twenty minutes after leaving her office.

Larry's poop-colored sheriffmobile sat in its usual spot, listing to port a little on a flat rear tire. Dammit, she'd *told* him to get a new spare for the damn thing!

His personal ride, a late Seventies Jeep CJ that rattled and clanked and would outlive them all, was missing.

So was the prowler's shotgun.

He only took it just in case. Nothing to worry about.

"Larry? You here, sugarbear?" She yelled as loud as she could without sounding like a crazy woman.

The only reply she got was the soft breeze rustling through the leaves.

And a joyful *yarkyarkyark* from the fenced-in yard behind the house. Skinner, Larry's redbone hound dog. And Joanie's second-favorite male on the planet.

Sending up a quick thank you to whoever listened to such things, Joan gripped the old-fashioned skeleton key Larry had given her. She almost ran for the door, but managed to keep herself to a quickstep instead.

Wouldn't be able to look for Larry if she broke an ankle, now would she?

"Larry? Sugarbear?"

The door opened onto the empty kitchen, still full of the morning's breakfast aromas.

The lights were off. The stove cold.

Skinner barked like a maniac from the back yard.

Joan moved slowly through the house, hand on her weapon even though she could feel the house's emptiness.

Nothing to see here, ma'am. Move along.

A wave of dizziness flooded through her head. That never happened to her, but her lover had never disappeared before, either.

She fell into the sofa and leaned her head back, breathing in through her nose, out through her mouth.

Her pulse beat against her chest and temples with a hammer, and spots flashed all throughout the room.

He'll be fine, Joan Foyle. Just fine.

The room shrank slowly down until it was just a bright pinprick of light.

Then it disappeared.

God, if you're there…if you're…

Chapter 5

"Whoo! *There* you are, young lady. Lordy, don't that sleep song take it plumb out of a body?"

What in the world?

Joan opened her eyes. She was still on the sofa. *A* sofa, anyway. But this one felt like canvas and heavy hair stuffing, not like Larry's vinyl and foam throwback.

Throwback? That was rich.

She looked around a living room both familiar and strange. No light fixture hung overhead. No lamps stood on the low tables.

And someone was moving around in Larry's kitchen.

Someone definitely *not* Larry.

"Who's there?" she called in her best cop voice, unsnapping the strap over her Sig Sauer .357. "This is Trooper Foyle of the Virginia State—"

"Joan Evelyn Foyle! You stop all that caterwaulin' and get yore tail in here! Our Lar-Bear needs us, and we ain't got a world o' time."

No matter how old she got or how many citations and awards she earned, hearing all three names like that made her feet move whether she wanted them to or not.

Besides, who else besides her called Larry Lar-Bear? He'd told him it started with—

And there she was.

Joan stepped into a kitchen from the great long ago, filled with fruit crate cabinetry, a heavy cast-iron wood-burning cookstove that put out more heat than the average volcano, an ancient, curvy-fronted icebox with a huge chrome latch handle like a meat locker.

And one extremely old woman in a blue calico dress and matching sunbonnet, sitting at Larry's butcher-block table, fanning herself with a newspaper with one gnarled, spotted hand and holding a smoking corncob pipe to her mouth with the other.

"Miz Crabtree?" Joan whispered. "Is that you?"

"'Course it's me," she said with a snort and a twinkle. "What a dang fool question. Now you got to sit and listen, Joanie. Putting the sleep in your eyes about did for me, and I can't stay long. Larry's on up to the Davis home, and he needs ye."

The strength went out of Joan's legs, and she fell into a chair. If she'd known, she would have realized it was the same chair Larry always used on visiting nights.

"What happened, ma'am? Where's Larry?"

A huge puff of blue smoke traveled ahead of Pearlie's answer.

"He's got himself lost, is where. And hurt. I can't see all of it, mind, but I know he found a cave on the hill just east of the Davis house. He's down inside the earth somewheres, and can't pick his way out. Mebbe he ain't got no light no more."

"Oh shit. I've got to get a crew together. I've got to call the spelunkers we use for underground rescue. I've got—"

"You got to calm yourself down, honey girl," Pearlie said softly, reaching across the table to take her hand. "You got all the rescuin' tools you need right here. You got what's 'twixt your ears, and you got a right fine hound dog tryin' to break the windows with that voice o' his. Twixt the two of ye, I reckon you can get to Larry before ary cave or coal crawler could."

Pearlie sat back, breathing heavily. She seemed...*thin*, somehow. Like she wasn't *there* so much as she had been.

"I'm sorry, honey girl. Sorry as all get out. But I can't stay. I'm used up, at least for a while. You go on now. Load up that dog and hie on over to the Davis place. Find that cave hole, and find my Lar-Bear. *Our* Lar-Bear."

Now the whole kitchen had gone as wispy as a movie projected on fog.

"Wait! How did...I mean, how am I here? I thought only Larry could..."

A huge smile, one twin to the smile that so warmed her heart when a younger man wore it, spread across the ancient, seamed face under the bonnet.

"Why, honey girl. Ain't you family now? I reckon you are, sure."

Chapter 6

JOAN JERKED AWAKE, her head snapping up so fast she was afraid a muscle relaxer might be in her future.

She wanted to believe it had been nothing but a strange dream brought on by stress.

Only it had been so *real.* And she never fell asleep out of the blue like that. And never woke up like she'd never gone to sleep at all.

Cave. She'd need light.

Joan scrambled up and ran to the kitchen, now hung with hemlock cabinets and missing the *Antiques Roadshow* appliances.

She rifled the drawers, snatching up every light she could find, even a couple of stubby emergency candles. She had her own light, of course. A heavy, LED Maglite with fresh batteries that should be good for a few hours, but had no intention of risking the pitch-black experience of a deep cave if she could help it.

Grabbing Skinner's twenty-foot retractable leash from its hook, she threw open the back door, and nearly hit the floor when fifty pounds of slobbery hound dog hit her legs.

"Skinner! Down!"

The hound's butt hit the floor automatically. Damn good thing Larry'd had the K9 crew work with the rambunctious ball of energy.

"Now listen, Skinner. You and me are going after your daddy, okay? I'm going to need your help."

Skinner panted his amiable agreement, sweeping the floor with his thick tail.

She clipped on his lead and walked him out to her car. She even let him ride up front as she melted asphalt all the way up Sandy Ridge to the Davis land.

Chapter 7

No one was home.

Tall poplar and oak trees surrounded a yard full of old engine bits, broken lawn furniture, and a kettle grill full of tall weeds.

Joan shut the unmarked Crown Vic off and got out, holding the end of Skinner's leash as he bounded past her to study the local botany, watering where necessary.

Three cars were parked in the grass-covered gravel in front of Floyd Davis' run-down gray, paintless farmhouse.

A rustbucket truck that might be an elderly Chevy.

A shiny new Charger, as orange as a hunter's toboggan.

And a vintage Jeep CJ. One that would rattle and clank and outlive them all.

She should clear the house. Look for Floyd or Gary or whoever.

But something told her no one was inside.

Not in the house, anyway.

"C'mon, boy. Find Daddy. Find Larry."

Skinner's head whipped up and he gave her a long stare, mouth closed for a change and with the look of a soldier who'd just gotten his orders.

And then he was off, nearly pulling her off her feet, heading for a narrow footpath at the edge of the trees.

He alternated between snuffling the ground and tasting the air, working back and forth in a zigzag as he narrowed down the scent trail.

God, if you're there, please let Skinner's nose be true.

He led/dragged her nearly a quarter mile up the track while she noted the lack of weeds and the well-packed dirt of the trail.

A shill *yark* split the air, and Skinner went to work at long tangle of kudzu vines blanketing a steep shelf of the ridge.

Joan let his leash spool up as she joined him. She felt a breeze from the other side of the vines, and pushed aside a thick hank to reveal a round hole in the hillside. A hole that stank of ammonia and rotten eggs.

"Good boy, Skinner!"

She gave his ears a quick rub as she studied the opening. Nearly as tall as she was, the hole didn't look quite natural. She was pretty sure it had been expanded over the years, although the walls inside looked like native rock.

She took a deep breath, checked her pockets for the spare flashlights, and turned her own on.

"Okay, Skinner boy. Go find him. Go find Larry. Go on, now."

She let him run out about eight feet of lead before locking it down and following his rotating tail into the darkness.

Chapter 8

Joan had to hunch over for a few yards, before the narrow passage opened up into a round chamber about fifteen feet across and eight high.

Not much water dripped from the ceiling, and Joan blessed the dry weather as she checked out a row of wooden tables covered with all the gear needed to cook up the latest bootlegger product.

None of the burners were lit, and only a dusting of residue was visible in the burners. Empty two-liter plastic bottles sprouted tubing, and a plastic trashcan near one of the benches was nearly full of broken batteries and empty cold pill boxes.

Overhead, vent holes had been dug through the cavern's ceiling. Flickering daylight came down through the cheap fans that sucked the worst of the fumes away.

Dammit. If any of these damn tweakers had done anything to her sugarbear…

Skinner sneezed a few times, nearly bouncing his

nose off the muddy floor, but he kept on, dragging her toward a smaller hole at the rear of the makeshift lab.

She followed him inside. This tunnel looked far less adjusted, the walls rough and uneven, the ceiling studded with broken stalactites.

Bits of fallen rock littered the ground, and Joan set every foot carefully in the slick cave mud as Skinner snuffled his way forward.

She strained her ears, listening for any sound other than her own footsteps, Skinner's loud breathing, or the occasional drip from overhead.

They walked for what seemed like hours, but her watch said was only forty-five minutes. Skinner led her past tunnels on both sides of this one, turning up some, down others.

The floor had dried somewhere along the way, robbing Joan of any footprints that might help her back out of this maze.

Suddenly, Skinner stopped like he'd hit a wall.

His head came up, his nose pointing toward the ceiling like a well-trained cop's handgun.

His jowls flapped as he sucked in a hundred breaths a second.

And then he *did* pull her off her feet, jerking the leash from her hands and shooting forward with his *daddy's home* bark echoing off the walls until Joan thought her ears would implode.

Before she had time to get good and scared at being left alone, she heard a weak voice from just around the next bend.

"Hey there, Skinner boy. I'm awful glad to see you."

Every muscle in her body relaxed as her eyes closed.

Larry. That was her man's voice. *Thank you,* whoever's listening!

Joan got to her feet and moved as fast as she dared through the rubble until she made it to the bend.

Her flashlight danced over Larry's pinched face, and he squinted her way with a tight, pained smile.

"Hey, Joanie. What's a nice gal like you doing in a place like this?"

"Looking for my idiot mate, of course." She rushed over to where he sat, his back against the tunnel wall and his legs stretched out in front of him. "The one who knows better than to head underground without letting people know what he's up to."

He closed his eyes, wincing as he leaned his head back, propping it against the hard stone.

She did a visual check. No blood, which was good.

But his left foot wasn't at the right angle.

She slid her hand gently down the leg toward his ankle, stopping when he hissed in a sharp breath.

"Damn stupid thing," he said, gripping her hand tight enough to squeeze the blood out of her fingers. "Wasn't watching my feet. Stepped on a rock the wrong way, and *snap.* I think maybe it's broke, Joanie."

Her eyes prickled and her chest drew tight, but she didn't have time for that foolishness.

"That's bad, Lar-Bear. But it could be a hell of a lot worse. Think you can walk on one leg if I prop you up?"

"I think so, yeah. Sure am thirsty. You didn't bring any water, did you? Or maybe a good stiff shot of bourbon or three?"

A laugh snuck out, surprising her as she helped him lever his way upright.

"Sorry, sugarbear. I left my cocktail kit in the car.

Come on, now. Put your arm over my shoulder and follow the wall with your other hand."

They got themselves arranged as best they could. Now how were they going to find their way out of here? Skinner had followed Larry's scent in, but…

She had an idea, and reached into her pocket for her car keys.

"Skinner! Hey, Skinner boy, want to go for a ride? In the car?"

She jangled the keys, and Skinner *yarked* happily, and began pulling them back the way they'd come.

It took nearly three times as long to escape the meth cave, and the moonless night was nearly as dark as the innards of the mountain by the time Joan and Larry finally pushed through the screen of kudzu and out into the fresh air.

As they hobbled toward the car, Larry told her how he'd found the cave.

"Got a whiff of the devil as soon as I got here, and just followed my nose."

Gary and some other tweaker Larry didn't know had been smoking their little hearts out in the lab room. One look at the brown badge man invading their secret clubhouse, and they'd bolted deeper into the cave. Larry hadn't seen any lights, and had no idea where they'd fetched up.

Chapter 9

Which wasn't a problem. It only took twelve hours and half the amateur spelunkers from the county cave-diving club to track them down, about half a mile under the mountain. Half-dead from dehydration and withdrawals, they'd cried like toddlers, ratting out a dozen dealers and houses as the rescuers led them out to a waiting screened-in back seat.

Joan sat by Larry's hospital bed, holding his hand as she studied the signatures that covered his cast.

"Doc Phipps says the break's clean," she said, kissing his fingers.

"That's right," came the Doc's voice from the doorway. She wondered how the old doctor who'd birthed half the town's grayhairs always sounded both amused and bored at the same time.

He carried a clipboard covered with arcane medical scribbling to the end of the bed, checking Larry's toes for color. "You'll have a limp you can tell lies about for a few months, but this time next year you'll never know you'd been that stupid."

"Thanks, Doc," Larry said, rolling his eyes at Joan. "I love how I can always count on you for your comforting words."

Doc Phipps wrote something on his clipboard, then opened a tall door in the cabinets lining one wall, pulling out a pair of aluminum crutches.

"You want comfort? Then let Trooper Foyle here give you a ride home. While she's at it, she can get that smelly hound dog out of my office. Going to take me a week to de-hair the place."

"Doc, you ain't nothin' but an old softie," Larry said as he struggled to his feet. He got the crutches settled in his armpits, tried a couple of exploratory steps, then held his hand out.

"Thanks a million, Doc. And sorry about the dog hair. I'll have Pauline send over a crate of lint rollers."

Doc Phipps waved a hand as he headed back out toward his other victims.

"Ah, that's all right, I suppose. It was good to have some intelligent company for a while."

Larry laughed, and Joan's heart lifted up a little bit.

"Come on, sugarbear. Let's get you home and settled in on the sofa. Aunt Joanie will bring you snacks and apple juice until your boo-boo is all better."

"Sounds good, sugarplum." Larry leaned forward, wrapping her up in the best hug he could without dropping his crutches.

"Maybe when I get this cast off, we might could get married? I mean, if you want to."

Joan's eyes nearly fell right out of her head, but the pump in her chest gave an unexpectedly happy little jump.

Not that this big oaf needed to know that.

"I'll think about it," she said, returning his hug and

adding a kiss. "But only if you promise to try and grow a brain in that head of yours."

"Deal. Gonna take a while, though. I think those pills the doc gave me are starting to kick in."

She laughed again, promising herself she'd have a long talk with Larry about his Granny once his head was on straight, and helped him into the wheelchair she'd use to roll him out to her car. Doc Phipps was heading their way down the hall, looking a little bit guilty as Skinner licked his lips and stared up at him with love and forbidden-food lust in his eyes.

God, if you're there…

No. Granny Pearlie, if *you're* there, thank you. Thank you for helping me bring my man out of the ground in one piece.

"Come on, boys. Let's go home."

JASON A. ADAMS
Author of Sunlit Dispositions
A REAL HERO

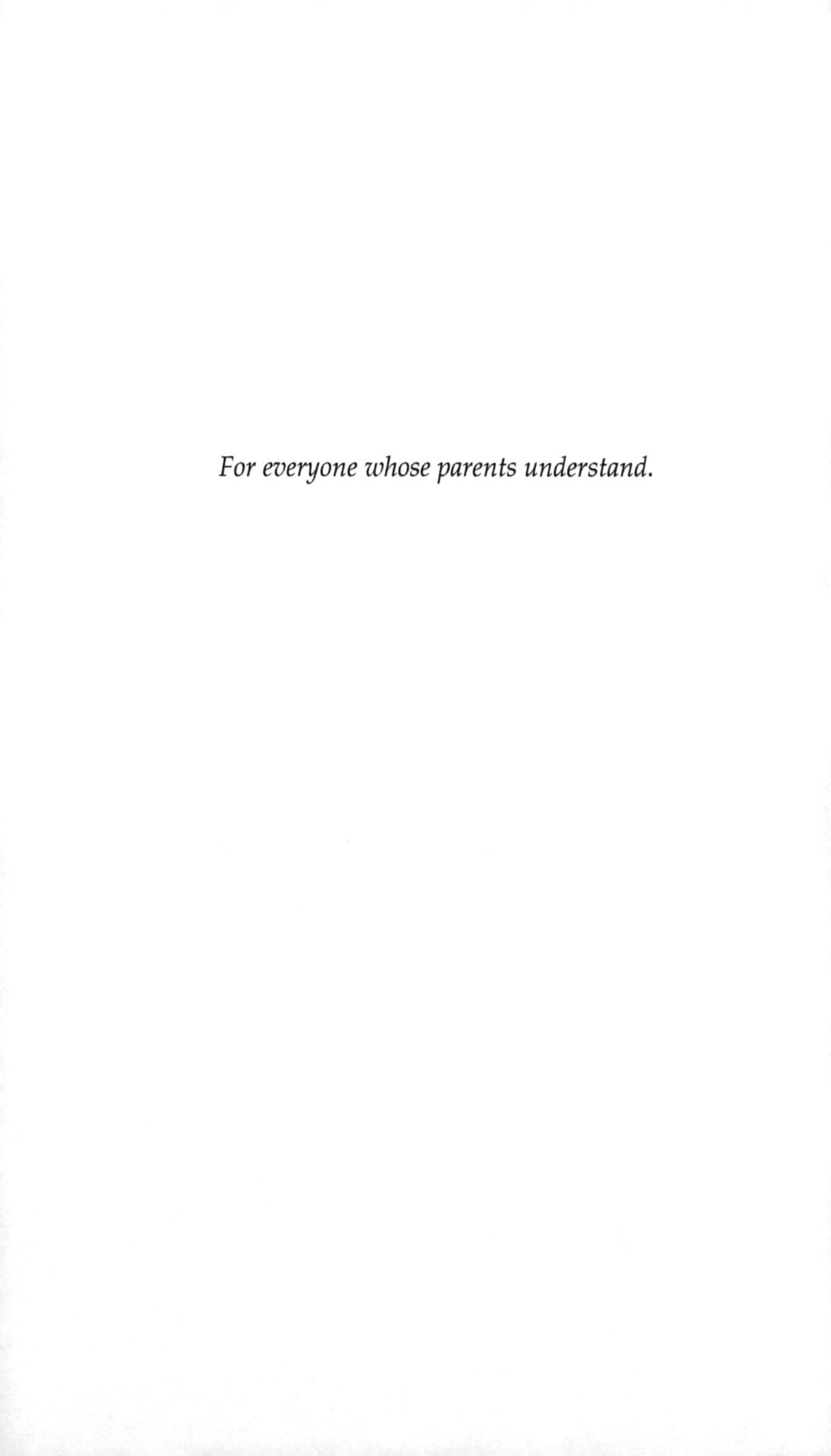

For everyone whose parents understand.

Chapter 1

Sometimes, heroism isn't where you first might think.

Jonlor Napier knew one thing for sure. *He* was no hero. And he should know.

He ate breakfast with a bona-fide hero most mornings. A hero he'd studied in school, been interviewed about to ascertain how the warmth of proximity to such a heroic soldier felt, questioned about when he'd follow in his parent's mighty bootsteps…

Blah blah blah.

Birds chirruped and sang in the trees of the family mango orchard. The sweet aroma of nearly-ripe fruit wafted in through the open patio doors on a warm, humid breeze designed by a benevolent deity (or more likely dialed in by a well-tipped climate manager) and perfect for spending a day flat on one's back under a tree, lazing in the sunshine and spinning out a new story or two.

Not that the son of the greatest military leader ever to come out of Xantares IV would be lollygagging or yarning. The son of such a man would be in school, learning all about tactics, astromath, personnel management, and so on and so forth and such like. It was only to be expected of a member of the family squadron.

And how could Jonlor safely break ranks when his dad was Defense Commander Tosach Joncar Napier, the Panther of the Pleaides?

DefCom Napier, darling of the newsvids, subject of a dozen entertainment reels, sat on Jonlor's right, working his way through an enormous stack of flapjacks and spicy, herbed soysage, his ribbon-encrusted scarlet jacket ("dyed in the blood of our enemies," so saith the recruiting posters) safely draped over the back of one ridiculously ostentatious chair carved from a single black and densely grained ebonut log.

All six chairs and the mirror-polished table they surrounded had come from the same tree, harvested from under the very noses of the rabidly warlike Tharhoons, a species of three-meter tall, six-limbed insectoids who wielded obsidian axes in each claw-tipped hand and mercilessly butchered any foolish visitor to their lava-soaked planet unfortunate enough to fall into their bloodthirsty clutches.

At least that's what the decorator who designed the dining room had said. Jonlor had seen the DefCom's smirk, and had his doubts.

The DefCom was home for two whole months this time, before leaving for another half-year of carrier duty aboard his flagship, the *Xerxes*, where he'd lead every patrol, flying his own fighter scout. Rank hath its privileges, and one of the DefCom's was a guarantee of flight status, regularly exercised.

Lorem, Jonlor's pop, bustled in and sat, the gleaming silvery lapels of hir formal burgundy jacket announcing that today would be a day with a Big Meeting.

Lorem lived for Big Meetings. Ze was a senior partner at Magellan Financial, an interquadrant banking empire that controlled more territory and resources than a dozen nearby stellar system governments. *Combined*, as Lorem was fond of saying.

With two such parents, Jonlor felt about as useful as a handful of dead mice in an underwear factory.

The DefCom might be the hero of the family, but Lorem was the chief bread-winner. Hir skill at negotiating trade deals had purchased not only the table, but also the huge villa that contained it. Built from genuine stone blocks quarried from marble and granite pits throughout Xantares, the house was an arched and becolumned testimony to Napier greatness.

Lorem spent at least a little time between every duty tour fussing at the DefCom for leaving his boots in the middle of the hall, his flight jacket and scarf hanging on the bannister in the great room, or his empty dishes and glasses on the sitting room rug for "those insufferable dogs."

One of said insufferables—Isolde, a fifteen kilo flop-eared no-breed of black shagginess named for one of Jonlor's favorite stories—sat at Jonlor's feet, graciously accepting the bits of flapjack he fed to her under the table.

Lorem didn't like that, either. And said so.

A soft chime from the gilt cockatoo in the center of the table announced that it was time to stop eating and go their various ways.

The DefCom wiped his mouth with his napkin and set his plate on the floor for Isolde, earning a *tsk* from Lorem.

As he shrugged on his uniform jacket, he gave Lorem a quick kiss and told hir to knock 'em flat in the meeting.

"And how about you, son?" he said, turning to Jonlor. "Any big plans for the school day? Counting the minutes to graduation, yet?"

"Nothing much, Sir," Jonlor said, checking his pockets for keys and compupad. "I'm Officer for the Day, so I guess I'll inspect the cadets this afternoon."

He hated OD days. He barely felt responsible for himself. Why trust him with responsibility for a couple-dozen classmates?

The DefCom adjusted his ribbon plate, easily wider than both of Jonlor's hands and topped with the system's only set of sparkling iridium wings. They rode even higher than the platinum starburst of his Honorable Service medal, of which the DefCom was the only living recipient.

No one who saw his chest had any doubts about his qualifications for the top job in the system's fleet.

"Don't forget to yell a little. Your buddies might gripe, but the Academy Commandant loves that silly shit." He ruffled Jonlor's hair and quick-marched to his personal transport, a tiny gyrocopter built by his own hands from archaic blueprints and not trusted to anyone else, even for engine maintenance.

As Jonlor watched the machine, which always reminded him a little of a dragonfly for some reason, Lorem rushed past him, brushing invisible dust from hir Monday-go-to-meeting jacket.

"Must dash," ze said. "*Big* meeting today. I'm hoping to secure the mining rights to the entire Tellorid system. *Big* money on the table. Do well in school today, and don't listen to your dad. Be firm with your cadets, of course, but don't forget to be fair. And don't forget to let me know how your Creativity assignment goes? It's a romantic adventure, yes?"

But Lorem dashed out to hir own vehicle, hir latest Rolls-Bentley groundcar, without waiting for an answer. Ze got a new one every year, probably spending enough on each to fund a couple of the DefCom's squadrons for the next war.

Still, Jonlor's pop always knew when he had a lit test, or got a story in the school e-pub.

Jonlor wondered if the DefCom even knew he could write at all.

He caught the autobus to school, knowing he wasn't being fair to his dad. After all, the DefCom had the welfare of an entire system on his mind. And Jonlor was a citizen, so by definition, the DefCom had *his* welfare on his mind as well.

Suuuure he did.

Chapter 2

"Jonlor, this is simply wonderful," Mister Meriweather, the Warrant Officer who taught Creativity said, wiping actual tears from her cheeks as she set the stack of paper on her blotter. "I'm hoping you'll let me submit it for this season's Chaucer Award in the youth author category."

"The Chaucer? Really?" Jonlor was stunned. *Real* writers submitted for the Chaucer Award for Excellence in Fiction, not underschool seniors who probably would be in Defense Scarlet before the ink on their diplomas dried.

"Absolutely. The way you evoke emotion, especially in the Flight Lead's homecoming with hir partner? Just lovely. And the pacing in the battle scene. I had to stop reading and catch my breath!"

She jotted a couple of lines on the back of his story. She always read stories on actual paper, not on screen. And she made her notes in red ink from a real writing pen.

She and the DefCom could have long-winded talks about ancient ways of doing things.

Not that Jonlor should talk. He'd been trying to teach himself Old and Middle English for the last six months, so he could read ancient stories in their native language.

"So, have you considered whether you will go to university after you graduate? Or where?"

The abrupt change of subject startled him.

"Um. I guess I'll probably enlist in the Defense Academy." His stomach clenched, as it always did.

Mister Meriweather studied him the way she'd study a questionable manuscript.

"Are you sure, Jonlor? I'd rather hoped you'd consider my old school, the Aeneid College for Creative Minds."

He *had* considered the Aeneid. Of course he had. He'd read every word on their net site. Had half the course catalog memorized. He'd even daydreamed about which order he'd take which classes in. But…

But.

He straightened up in his best cadet ten-hut, clenching his fists against himself.

"I don't want to dishonor my father by not enlisting, Mister Meriweather."

She sighed. "I know you'd never dishonor either of your parents, Jonlor. Now you'd best be going, or you'll be late for your next class." She waved a hand, dismissing him.

But as he reached the door, she called after him.

"Although I think you'd be surprised at what *dishonor* means to the Defense Commander."

Chapter 3

Jonlor lay on his bed, enjoying the feel of the cool neocotton sheets against his skin. Woven from strands finer than silk and weight-for-weight worth more than naturally mined rubies, their softness—and the decadent gel mattress beneath—were a luxury he'd never admit to Lorem how much he enjoyed.

At the Aeneid College for Creative Minds, you'll learn how to transfer the words and images in your head to the grateful denizens of a thousand worlds.

The dim glow of his compupad offered the only light in his otherwise pitch-black bedroom. He didn't worry about tripping on anything if he had to visit the lavatory. After eighteen years living under the watchful eye of the DefCom, and the even more watchful eye of the slightly-more-anal-than-an-anus Lorem, Jonlor never left so much as a tissue not in its proper place.

The Aeneid. A college specifically chartered for Creative Minds. The school that produced the best writers, playwrights, sculptors, painters, vid actors, and directors…

He tossed the pad aside, the glow disappearing among the rumpled sheets.

Mister Meriweather had indeed entered his story in the Chaucer. Judging would be any day now.

He rolled over, checked the time. Three-thirty. He really needed to catch a couple of hours of sleep or he'd be useless at school tomorrow. Later today. Whatever.

Would he manage to place in the awards? Or would the judges print his story as Mister Meriweather had, simply so they could burn it?

He snatched up his pad again, flicking the screen to another page.

The entrance application for the Aeneid.

Guilt, hope, fear. All of it chased through his brain like a squirrel on uppers, filling his stomach with a rolling mix of acid and cramps.

He thought of the DefCom. Of his dad. Of watching him speechify to a quadrangle filled with soldiers and pilots, all of them cheering every time he paused for breath. Of his stern face, so unlike the face he wore at home, on a million screens in a million households across the system, reporting on the state of defense.

The system hadn't been at war since Jonlor first learned how to operate the lavatory for himself, but regular defense reports still filled the screens on the first of every month.

He saw himself in a scarlet jacket. Bossing juniors about. Filling out reports. Spending half his life on board some ship or other

He also pictured himself in an expensively tailored

suit, lapels reflecting the light as he drove a hard bargain against a bevy of obstinate trading partners.

And he thought about all the people who lived inside his imagination. Of all their stories, and how hard he tried to do them justice.

Who was he kidding? He'd be lucky to make the list of entrants for the Chaucer. And acceptance to the Aeneid? That was for actual artists. People who could really be creative, not just for kids whose Creativity teachers happened to be the DefCom's subordinates.

But.

But.

He thought about all those ribbons on the DefCom's jacket. All the decorations and commendations for bravery. For courage in battle.

Jonlor pressed his thumbprint to the bottom of the Aeneid application screen, and hit submit.

Chapter 4

SCHOOL WENT by in a foggy haze.

Jonlor had managed an hour of semi-doze, filled with half-dreams of success. And of failure. And worst of all, of disappointment. His own, and his parents'.

He couldn't wait to be an adult. No matter what career awaited him, he might at least finally feel like he knew what he was doing.

He managed to stay awake through all his classes. Mostly, anyway. But he did manage a short nap on the autobus ride home.

And wondered if he was still asleep when he walked into the house.

Lorem and the DefCom stood in the middle of the great hall, surrounded by more than a dozen others.

All his teachers were there.

And Colonel Perkins, the Academy Commandant. Colonel Perkins had to be in his eighth decade, but he stood straight as an arrow in his dress scarlet. His ribbon plate wasn't quite so large as the DefCom's, but was still impressive.

All his instructors wore their scarlets. Except for Mister Meriweather, who wore a diaphanous gown, so sheer it must be real spidersilk.

All of them held glasses of sparkling amber liquid, and Jonlor smelled half a vat's worth of champagne in the large room.

As he stood in the great room's entryway, the entire company turned to him, raising their glasses in unison.

"To the winner of the Silver Quill Youth Author in the two-hundred and thirty-seventh Chaucer Award for Excellence in Fiction!" Mister Meriweather raised her glass higher as she made the toast, and everyone followed suit.

Even the DefCom, who wore a grin bigger than any Jonlor had ever seen.

Everyone drank, then everyone cheered.

Jonlor felt like his face had caught fire, and he was sure his own grin was big and dopey.

He'd won the Chaucer! With a story he wrote himself!

His parents came over and flanked him before he could figure out how to say anything.

"Work the room," Lorem whispered to him, dropping a wink. "Let everyone touch the royal majesty."

"They all came to throw you up on their shoulders," the DefCom whispered in his other ear. "Figuratively speaking, of course. So let 'em. You earned it, son. *Well* done!"

And for only the third or fourth time he could remember, Jonlor felt the DefCom's arms pull him in for a rough hug.

The party was nearly as fog-riddled as his school day had been. Everyone wanted to congratulate Jonlor.

And most seemed to have actually read his winning story.

The highlight of the whole thing was when Golden, the DefCom's aide de camp, pulled him into a warm, full-body embrace.

"It was a beautiful tale," ze said against the nuclear furnace of Jonlor's cheek. "I read the whole thing in an hour, then spent half the night filming the vid in my head. Thank you for creating such a piece, young Jonlor."

And then ze kissed him, right there in front of everybody.

Of all the laughs and whistles that followed, the DefCom's was the loudest.

Chapter 5

JONLOR'S SHOULDERS slumped as the door closed behind the last of the departing guests.

Between his sleepless night and the barrage of happy congratulating, he felt like he could sleep half the calendar away.

Once again, he sat at the huge ebonut table, with the DefCom on his right and his pop on the left. All three sipped from mugs of the DefCom's special gotta-stay-awake tea, although Jonlor didn't think it would do him much good tonight.

"We're just *so* proud of you, son," Lorem said, beaming like ze'd just bought out a competitor. "I knew you were a fine writer, but wow! The Chaucer! If you want any advice on what to do with the purse, I'm always here."

Same old pop, but Jonlor was grateful.

Jonlor breathed in. Breathed out. He had to tell his parents, tell them while there was still a chance to contain any damage.

"Pop? Sir? I need to tell you both something."

They put their serious-conversation faces on, but the DefCom's eyes had a twinkle that made Jonlor nervous.

"It's about…well…I've been thinking about what to do next. After graduation, I mean…"

His parents just watched him without saying a word.

They were no help. No help at all.

"And I think…I mean, I don't want to disappoint you, Sir. Or you, Pop. But I've applied to the Aeneid College for Creative Minds."

Two eyebrows on two faces rose.

"Not that they'll probably accept me. And I can always go to the Defense Academy, instead. I mean…"

The DefCom raised one hand. Jonlor had seen generals shut their mouths when that hand went up, and he wasn't any less susceptible.

"You've already been accepted by the governors of the Aeneid," the DefCom said quietly. "And by the Defense Academy's Officer Training School."

"And by the Magellan's business college," Lorem said, reaching over to take the DefCom's raised hand in hir own.

"I have? Huh? When?" All of Jonlor's carefully prepared defiance fizzled out like a match dropped in a bucket of water.

"Oh, son. You've been down for the Magellan and the Academy since before you could walk." Lorem said, smiling at him. "Your natal scans showed a mind capable of remarkable talents, in a wide range of possible career paths."

"Plus," the DefCom said, "I've got all these pretty

bits of cloth and metal on my coat, and that seems to impress some people."

Lorem took one of Jonlor's hands with hir free one, and the DefCom took the other, completing the circle.

"And Mister Meriweather has been sending the Aeneid all the stories you write for class for some time now," Lorem went on. "The head of the Creative Fiction department thinks you have quite a future, and he promised to 'strive not to teach you enough to ruin your unique voice,' I believe is how he put it."

"So you have a choice to make, son," the DefCom said. "And only *you* can make it. Do you want to follow in my footsteps? Or those of your pop? Or do you want to start making footsteps of your own?"

Jonlor could only stare at his parents. At his pop, who dripped tears on hir mirrored lapels. At the DefCom—at his dad, who smiled as serenely as a monk on a mountaintop, the iridium wings on his scarlet chest flashing in the light.

"I don't know what to do," he finally admitted. "I've dreamed about the Aeneid, but I don't want to dishonor—"

Again that hand went up.

"Stop right there, Jonlor," his dad said. "Do you honestly think you could dishonor me, dishonor either of us, as long as you don't turn into some sort of criminal mastermind? *My* son just won one of the most prestigious creativity awards there is. *My* son just got accepted into the premier college for artists I've ever heard of. So don't you go accusing *my* son of dishonoring anybody, hear me?"

Lorem picked up where the DefCom left off.

"And I spend my days listening to liars and storytellers from here to Old Earth. It would be nice to read lies and stories meant to entertain instead of swindle."

Jonlor's dad let go of his hand, tapped the back with a calloused finger.

"People call me a hero, but I don't see myself as one. I put on the uniform for one reason, and that's because I wanted to fly. I had the bad luck to join up right before the Pleiades War, and got shipped out to the lines when I was younger than you are."

His smile was back, but this time it was the hard smile he showed the troops, not his easy at-home grin.

"I got damned lucky, and survived. I was no *hero*, believe me. I was a shit-scared kid doing my best to stay alive, and to help my buddies when they got in a scrape. The *Panther of the Pleiades*, as all those silly people tagged me, spent half the war trying to scrub shit out of his britches."

He laughed, and Jonlor was surprised by his own matching laugh.

"I'll tell you something about heroes, son. Heroes are people who do what needs doing, no matter how terrified they might be."

"I can't tell you how scared I was during my first financial presentation," Lorem said, smiling. "I mean, my hands shook so badly I was hanging on to the podium like a drowning child with a life preserver. I still get butterflies before a big meeting."

They both took Jonlor's hands again before the DefCom went on.

"So the question now is what needs doing, son? Do you *need* to be a soldier? Or a businessperson?"

"Or do you *need* to be a storyteller?" Lorem asked gently. "The galaxy has plenty of soldiers, and plenty of financial executives."

"Of course there are plenty of storytellers too," his dad said, squeezing Jonlor's hand. "But there are never *enough* storytellers. You want to be a hero like your dad, son?" He winced when he said hero, but kept going. "If you want to be a hero, then give people a way to escape their day-to-day lives. Give people a window into that wonderful imagination of yours."

Jonlor looked from his dad to his pop. Saw the love and acceptance and pride in their eyes.

He tried, but it took him nearly five minutes to squeeze any words out past the lump in his throat.

"I can go to the Aeneid? Really I can? And you won't mind?"

Now both of his parents squeezed his hands.

"Son," his dad said. "If you want to make me proud, if you want your poor old dad to think you're a *real* hero, then you'll do whatever it is that will bring *you*—and all your future readers—the most joy. Personally, I think that means a few years of dorm food at some crazy creativity school, but it's up to you."

"We've never *not* been proud of you, Jonlor," Lorem said, a suspicious glint at the corners of hir eyes. "And I for one can't *wait* to read your next story, if you'd do me the honor of allowing me."

Jonlor's own eyes felt a bit watery as he got up to hug his pop, and then his dad.

"Thank you. Thank you so much," he said, shaking Lorem's hand like he'd seen others do, then standing to attention and saluting the DefCom.

"Would you please knock that silly shit off?" he said in a gravelly growl. "I get enough of that around the squad room."

Jonlor laughed as he wiped his eyes with his palms.

He was already planning what all to take to college with him.

And what story he would write for Lorem. Something romantic. Maybe another yarn involving a dashing hero of the stars and the object of hir desire.

What a story it would all make.

JASON A. ADAMS
Author of Agonist and To Catch a Thief

FREEING THE SPIRIT

For everyone who steps in.

Chapter 1

Aʜ, the farming life. Salt of the earth. Bound to the soil. Stewards husbanding nourishment from the bosom of Mother Nature.

How Irene Sandifur hated it.

No one in the movies ever had to scrub pig shit out of the seat of their favorite jeans. Or talked about how a hot day after the field had been fertilized meant tears and snot running like a river all night. How they could *taste* chicken manure after a day mucking out the barn.

Or how their parents would raid hoarded allowance and prize money to pay for repairs on the combine, their most beloved child. Her grandmother was the only one that ever saw her as more than another tool on the farm, but the big C had taken her out when Irene was only eight. She shared her first name Yvonne with Grandma, but no one ever called her that. Only by her middle name. *Irene.* Ick.

She wished she'd been a beatnik like Grandma back in the day. Doing her own thing. Hanging out in the Village with cool cats and hep kittens.

Farm life was so *boring*. Every day was the anniversary of exactly the same thing as last year.

Disk and plow. Plant and treat. Fertilizer this week, insecticide next week. Weed control. Check the soybeans. Check the weather. Help Daddy wrangle the irrigator and watch it roll along like the world's biggest Slinky, spraying liquid money over faded stalks that just had to turn green if she wanted to go on that next school trip.

She could always tell what time of year it was by what god-awful stink came from the fields.

The only thing that ever changed was her inseam measurement and bust size. And the band on the t-shirts she kept hidden away from her oh-so-pious parental units along with a fabulous pair of high-heeled pirate boots she'd saved up for weeks to get. No idea when she'd get a chance to wear them, since goth bands didn't play podunk farm towns all that often.

She stood up from the rack of tomato sprouts, clasping her hands in the small of her back and stretching until loud crackles ran all the way from her tailbone to her skull. She was still a little stiff from last night's Tae Kwon Do workout, but in a good way.

Daddy hated that his little girl was so into something so very unladylike, but her martial arts classes were the one thing she wouldn't back down on, no matter how much he yelled or how much her mother cajoled. Hard training and sparring kept the knot inside her at bay. Kept her from giving in whenever someone needed a good shot upside the head.

After six years, she was pretty good at it, if she did say so herself. And had the trophies to prove it.

At least seedling maintenance wasn't so bad. Irene had the greenhouse shed to herself. The Sandifur cash crop was soybeans, and didn't *that* just make the family stand out from a thousand other soybean farmers.

Irene handled all the sprouts for the for-us garden. Her favorite was squash, of course. You could pretty much fling a handful of zucchini or crookneck seeds over your shoulder and be swimming in squash until first frost.

Today was tomatoes, though. Brandywines for eating, and Biltmores for sauce and canning. Irene had eight dozen of each, all in miniature peat pots full of her own compost blend. A blend whose discovery had also led to the discovery of dish soap and peroxide for manure-stained jeans.

Not that she planned to be in the hothouse-tomato biz for much longer. She'd be graduating from Shallowford High in six weeks. She already had her own car, a beat-up 1972 Chevy Vega in charming shades of waxless orange mixed with gray primer she'd paid a hundred bucks for, and another one-fifty to patch up the engine enough to be more-or-less reliable.

The parental units hated the freedom Vicky Vega gave her, but she'd won the money fair and square, and she'd gotten it in cash. Cash which Daddy hadn't managed to squirrel away in the shoebox under the spare linens in his old army footlocker, like the rest of the family's unbanked funds.

One more summer of serfitude and drudgery, then she'd take Vicky and go off to…

Somewhere.

*Any*where besides Iowa. So long as she never got dirt under her fingernails again.

The best way she could think to celebrate putting Iowa and the 1900s in the rearview mirror was by finally moving to somewhere pigshit-free.

Chapter 2

Clouds had rolled in by the time she finished thinning the miniature plants in the greenhouse, and the setting sun cut underneath their black bulk with a gorgeous wash of bloody light almost the same color as Irene's waist-length waves of hair.

Everyone carried on about how pretty her hair was. How she must be *so* proud of it.

They'd never tried to drag a brush through the mess, either. But Daddy put his foot down whenever she talked about hacking off a foot or so. Crowning glory, blah blah.

Daddy's hair wasn't long enough to hide a flea. What the hell would he know about it?

She crossed the flat, pig-stomped yard to the house, wondering if she'd ever be able to pick it out of a lineup.

She'd gone with her best friend Cindy on a few pre-Census mapping gigs. Cindy was in Irene's class at school, but she'd already turned eighteen and signed up as soon as the fliers for census workers went up all over town.

The mapping was pretty easy. In a state shaped by Nature's belt sander during the Ice Age, no houses could hide.

And the description was always the same. White house, black shutters. White house, black shutters. White house, black shutters, and hey, a tire swing this time.

Her mouth watered at the smell of fried chicken coming from the range vent's exhaust hole. Her mother could be a pain, but she was an awfully good cook. Always got pestered for her recipes every time the Shallowford Love of Christ Church held a big feed in the gigantic picnic shelter that dwarfed the rickety clapboard church itself.

Her appetite flared, then shrank a little when she heard Daddy yelling at the TV set. Probably meant a Clinton speech or an Al Gore campaign ad. Daddy was a little to the right of Hitler, and thought Bubba Clinton was in bed with the commies.

Like, there hadn't been any commies to speak of since the Soviet Union fell apart eight years ago.

"Oh, there you are, Rennie dear." Her mother stood at her dutiful place, flipping bits of dead bird in a cast iron skillet. "You just have time to clean up and eat before Service. Best hurry along, now."

Shit. She'd almost managed to forget it was Wednesday. That was something else she wouldn't miss in the rearview mirror.

Irene stomped up to her room, wondering if she could manage a quick deadly bout of plague before church time. Probably not.

She *should* tell the units that she'd read their little book, and didn't believe a word of it. But she was still seventeen, which meant Daddy still had control of her bucks. Nearly two thousand, and she'd probably score another couple-hundred at the next martial arts meet in May.

She sighed as she shucked her jeans and pulled on the horrid gray skirt and frilly, shiny top that choked her neck and manacled her wrists with plastic pearl buttons. But she'd be damned if she was gonna braid her hair.

Just a few more months. That's all.

Chapter 3

IRENE MADE it through the service without nodding off once. Wasn't easy, even if Brother Phillip had a voice like a tractor with a bad transmission, and the annoying habit of breaking into gibberish noises whenever he wanted to impress the sheep with his holy-fied spirit.

Shorter than Irene's towering five-six, and with a gut that always made her wonder how much of the communion bread and grape juice he put away between services, B.P. was a jolly little Santa Claus. One who talked nonsense and pretended to wave fake illnesses away, but he put on a decent show, and always laughed at people's jokes.

Especially people who tithed well.

She spotted Joyce, one of her best friends and one of the few people who seemed to really *get* Irene. The units were all milling around the front of the sanctuary, trying to one-up each other in piousness.

"Hey, Joyce. You survive the bible beating?"

Joyce about bounced her head on the ceiling, she

jumped so bad. Her heavy black braid swung wildly as she whipped around to face Irene, and her own gray skirt twirled scandalously.

Irene wasn't overly scandalized. Joyce had awfully nice legs.

"Oh. Hi, Rennie. How are you?"

Joyce, who often sat with Irene giggling and pointing out unfortunate fashion choices among their poorly evolved classmates, looked like she hadn't slept in days. Dark circles under her eyes, skin paler than Irene's own in the middle of winter, and she looked several pounds lighter, and not in a healthy way.

Come to think of it, Irene hadn't seen her outside of school in a week. And even at school, she'd been keeping to herself.

Irene felt a guilty little pang somewhere deep down. She'd been so busy planning her own escape, she hadn't even bothered to notice her friend's...what? Decline?

"I'm good," Irene said. "Hey, want to go check out the picnic shelter with me?"

Without waiting for an answer, she grabbed Joyce's hand and pulled her outside, and out to one of the splintery wooden picnic tables.

At first, Joyce resisted. Then she seemed to give in, and let Irene drag her along like a doll.

"What's up, Joycie?" she asked. "You look like a wet mop. You feeling okay?"

Joyce looked everywhere but at Irene. Red spots bloomed on her cheeks as she ran her hands down her blouse, smoothing the perfectly smooth polyester.

"I'm fine, Rennie. It's just... I've been busy. I'm... helping Brother Phillip in the evenings."

"Helping him with what?" Weird. Joyce always

made fun of the pudgy, combed-over preacher man as much as she did herself.

"It's… He…he's helping me make some money for summer classes. At the community college."

"Oh yeah? What's the gig, gal? Maybe I can get in on it."

A warm breeze drifted across the rows of tables, carrying the smell of freshly turned soil, and more fertilizer. Joyce sneezed, but not hard enough to explain how red her blue eyes were.

"I'm… I don't want to talk about it, okay?"

Oh shit. Was B.P. some kind of pervo? Joyce wasn't a snowy innocent or anything. Irene had helped see to that herself on more than one sleepover. Something was up, though.

Irene took Joyce's hands in hers.

"What's going on, honey? What's he making you do for money? Is he—"

Joyce snatched her hands back and jumped to her feet.

"It's just some pictures, okay? It's no big deal. *And it's none of your business! Just leave me alone!*"

And Irene's best friend ran back to the church.

Back to Brother Phillips' kingdom.

Chapter 4

How to go about this.

Irene had tried to call Joyce, but her mom said she wasn't feeling well. Every single time.

After a dozen calls, she gave up. Joyce wouldn't talk to her. Probably not to anyone who knew her well enough to know something bad was up.

She tried to talk to her at school the next day, but every time she saw Irene, Joyce turned and walked away.

Once she got home, Irene had the incredibly stupid idea of trying to talk to her mother.

"Mom? What should I do if I think one of my friends is in some kind of trouble?"

"Hmm?" The mother unit was sitting at the kitchen table, busily hot-gluing plastic rhinestones to her scrapbook, lining them up with a wooden ruler, but at least she'd noticed Irene speak.

She sat down across from her, picked up an as-yet untrapped sparkly bit and started bouncing it on the table, catching it in her fingertips.

Her mother finally looked up, the line between her eyes deepening as it always did when yet another thing annoyed her.

"Stop that, Rennie. I'm trying to concentrate, and you're—"

"One of my friends is in trouble, Mom. Trouble with a man. An *older* man."

Her mother sniffed. Picked up another rhinestone. Blue, this time.

"If one of those girls is flipping her skirts, I don't want you spending time with her. Those girls are all bound for babysitters on graduation night, mark my words."

Irene felt the familiar knot of fire in her belly. The one she'd worked so hard at the dojo to tame.

"It's not her fault. She needs money, and I think this man is taking advantage of her."

"Then why doesn't she talk to her own parents? Or the police?"

Irene drew in a breath and dropped the bomb.

"Because it's Brother Phillips, Mom."

Irene never even saw her mother's hand, but she heard the flat *crack* and felt pain flare up in her cheek.

"Don't you *dare*, young lady! Don't you *dare* talk that way about Brother Phillips!" Through tears of shock and pain, Irene saw her mother stand up and raise her ruler over her head like a sword.

"He's a *good* man, and as close to The Lord as a man can be this side of the grave. Which one of those hussy *friends* of yours put that in your head?"

A quick roundhouse kick to the kidney.

Or an open-palm shot under the chin.

Maybe an elbow to the...

Irene clamped down, clenching her fists and telling the knot in her gut to wait, just wait.

"You know what? Just forget it," she said, flipping the gaudy plastic diamond back toward her mother's stupid scrapbook. "Doesn't matter. Maybe it would be better if no one paid attention, right? Just didn't talk about it, or notice anything's wrong. Right, Mom? Maybe that way he can finally get around to sending someone to graduation night with a babysitter. Right?"

She got to her feet, stiff as a board, but still in perfect control.

Brother Phillips would be at the church by now. He was always there in the evenings, in case any of the brethren or sistren needed his special guidance.

"I'm going out, Mom. I'm not sure what time I'll be home."

Irene was a little surprised at how calm she sounded to herself.

That ruler jabbed toward her chest.

"You will *not*. You're going to stay right here until your father comes in, and then you're going to tell him how you accused a godly man of sin, and you'll ask your father's forgiveness on your *knees* for being such a wicked liar."

"You know? I don't think I will. You're dripping, by the way."

Irene pointed at the glob of hot glue stretching from the gun's nozzle to the pleather scrapbook cover, then she turned around and started toward her room.

Her mother spluttered threats and dire consequences, but Irene didn't pay any attention.

Once in her bedroom with the door safely shut, and her bookcase shoved against the door for good measure, she studied her closet.

What to wear, what to wear…

Finally she settled on her TKD uniform pants, heavy cotton with lots of give in strategic places.

Next, she pulled on her pirate boots. The three-inch heel shouldn't be enough to cause her any problems, and the black pants tucked nicely down inside the calf-high shafts.

She considered putting on her Nine Inch Nails tee, but decided against it. Pity, Trent had the right attitude, but she should probably try for something a little less confrontational.

Like, say, the white frilly blouse she always wore to church. Only without the choker buttons done up. Or the bra.

She studied herself in the mirror over her dresser, liking what she saw. The boots gave her a bit more height, and the silly shirt actually worked with the black pants. With her bosom unstrapped, she felt… *Sexy.* Dangerous. And alive.

Still needed something though…

Irene pushed the bookcase away from her door, expecting a flaming mother to burst through like a righteous meteor.

No one was outside, though.

Her dad must've come in from the field early, or else her mother had fetched him. She could hear both units speaking in low, angry voices. Probably trying to figure out how to get a failed Pentecostal girl into a convent, or something.

She tiptoed across the hall to the units' room and opened her dad's closet.

Yep, there was his Sunday-go-to-funeral suit, still in the plastic bag from its annual trip to the dry cleaners in Des Moines.

Taking it from the hanger, she dumped everything but the one bit she wanted and went back to her own room to study herself in the mirror again.

A little tight in the tits, but the black vest simply *made* the outfit.

Time to go see if she could get some modeling work.

Chapter 5

Like she figured, the lights at the church were on when she pulled into the parking lot, Vicky Vega rocking and gronking on bad springs and worse shock absorbers as she came to a stop.

And Vicky was the only car in the lot.

She got out. Checked herself in Vicky's side mirror. Popped another button on her blouse.

The sanctuary door was unlocked, of course. Gawd would never let a thief invade. Didn't Brother Phillips always talk about how they all had to trust in The Plan?

She went in, walking up the aisle toward the back, where another door led to B.P.'s tiny office.

And there was the pudgy little toad. Sitting behind his desk. Staring at something on his computer, one hand in his lap.

Creepster.

Irene knocked on the door jamb, and the creepy toad nearly shit himself. Very gratifying.

"Oh, hello Irene," he said, smiling like a man with a

lemon in his ass. His hand moved, and she heard a zipper. "What brings you here, young lady?"

She tried a simper. Too bad she hadn't practiced, but what can you do?

"Hi, Brother Phillips. I…um…was wondering if you had any…um…*work* I could do? I'm going to be short on my tuition for college next fall. Joyce said… said that you might…um…"

She tried a smile next. The same smile her mother used whenever she had to ask her dad for permission to buy something.

The Toad stopped smiling. Now he looked like someone who'd just been offered candy from a stranger.

"And what did young Joyce tell you, exactly?"

"Nothing much, sir. Just something about pictures?"

She walked in and sat in his visitor's chair, hands on the arms so the top of her blouse spread a little.

The Toad's eyes flicked down, then back up.

"What do your parents say? Do they mind if you work for me?"

"Oh I didn't tell them yet, sir. I wanted to talk to you first. They don't even know I'm here." She widened her eyes and tried for worried. "You won't tell them, will you sir? I don't want them to say no before you can say yes."

He leaned back, letting his gut rise up over the edge of the desk like a dumply rising sun.

"I am always looking for…ah…models. For the annual church fundraiser calendar, of course. I *could* take a few test photos, I suppose. See how the camera treats you."

Now Irene smiled. A real smile, this time.

Sucker.

"That would be *great,* sir! Can we do it right now?"

He drummed his fingers on the desk and squinted at her. Those beady little eyes flicked down again.

"Why not? Why don't you stand against the wall there, and I'll get the camera ready."

Irene dutifully rose and stood against the wall, under the silly Jesus clock everyone in town seemed to have. *Jesus, would you look at the time?*

"Like this, sir?"

She put her hands behind her, leaning back against the wall, pointing her tits at him like a pair of cannons.

Well, pistols, maybe.

The Toad had taken up a Polaroid One-Step on a tripod from where it leaned in the corner. He looked up to check her pose, and almost knocked the camera over.

Shit, were all men this easy to mess with?

"That's…that's good, Irene. Now smile like a good girl. That's it…one second…"

The camera flashed. A photo rolled out with a *chicka-zzzz.*

"Now let's see how it looks," the Toad said, waving the gray blankness as it slowly turned into a picture.

"Let me see," Irene said, coming over to stand *very* close to him, her shoulder ever-so-accidentally bumping his.

You know, she didn't look half bad. Even Jesus would have looked down if he wasn't so obsessed with the time.

"Very nice," the Toad said. Sounded to Irene like he was breathing a little heavy. "Want to try a couple more?"

"You bet, sir. You can take all the pictures of me you want."

She skipped back to the wall. Not an easy thing to do in her boots, but she managed it.

"Irene..."

His face had gone a bit blotchy, and he kept wiping his hands on his pants.

"Yes sir?"

"You're a beautiful young lady, Irene. I'd like to take a few more pictures. Ones that capture the gift of beauty God has given you."

She made her eyes all big and googly again.

"What do you mean, Brother Phillips? Can you show me?"

"Of course. Now don't be afraid..."

He came toward her. Irene relaxed her arms and legs. Tightened her abs.

"Just let me—"

As soon as he reached for her buttons with his toady hands, Irene brought her knee up. *Hard*. Right into probably the world's tiniest package. She followed that with a double-clap to his waxy ears, then grabbed his head and brought it down so he could kiss her other knee.

She'd have to get some peroxide on the way home, before the blood on her pants could set.

The Toad didn't croak on the way down. Except for the first surprised grunt, he didn't make a sound. Just went straight off to la-la land.

Irene's pulse raced and she felt heat in her cheeks.

She stared down at the inert lump at her feet.

She felt like she could *fly*.

And she would, but not yet. First she had to arrange things.

The Toad's desk was unlocked, except for the bottom right-hand drawer. She glanced at the computer screen, made a face at what she saw, then went back to rummage through the Toad's pockets until she found his keys.

What an idiot. He kept all his pictures right there. In envelopes with the *model's* names written on each.

Disgusting.

Irene dumped the pictures all over the Toad, dousing him with teenaged skin. Then she called the cops.

"No, I can't give you my name. Just send someone to the Love of Christ Church. And hurry. I think Brother Phillips had a heart attack."

He at least had a broken nose. And probably he'd be pissing blood for a few days.

She left the church door open as she went back to Vicky, the envelope marked *Joyce* in her back pocket and on its way to a hot date with some lighter fluid.

Chapter 6

By the next day, the whole town was buzzing with the news.

Did you hear? Pictures of naked girls. Poor Dick and Janet, their young Nancy. FBI came. Took everything at the church.

Feeling just a teensy bit smug, Irene got home from school, limping a little. Her left knee had one beauty of a bruise. And a couple of tooth marks.

Both her parental units sat at the kitchen table. Her mother had a stack of flyers, and handed a sheaf to her as she sat down.

"Take these to school tomorrow, honey. Make sure you put one on every bulletin board."

Irene took the papers. Smug slowly turned to outrage as she read.

CHARITY DINNER AND AUCTION!

Please join us at the Shallowford Love of Christ Church picnic shelter every night this week, where we will be selling hot dinners and auctioning items donated by the faithful to raise funds for the defense of our beloved Brother Phillips as he faces…

"You've got to be *kidding*," she said, staring at first her mother, then her father. "A *defense* fund? For that pedo toad?"

"He's *not* a pedophile!" her father shouted. "Someone's trying to destroy a good man, and all of us are going to help him overcome this. *Including* you, young missy."

"What about all the pictures?" Irene said, slinging the flyers back toward her mother. They scattered, most of them sliding off the table and fluttering to the floor.

"Fakes," her mother said, sniffling and dabbing at her eyes. "Horrible fakes. Those poor girls."

Irene couldn't believe this shit.

"His fingerprints were all over them," she said. Probably true.

"No, they weren't," her mother said as her father shook his head. "Of course they weren't. Or if they were, it's all part of how they're trying to frame him."

"Who's 'they?'"

"I don't know," her father snapped. "Someone who can't stand to see a good, Godly man stand for the people of his community. I won't hear one more peep out of you, Irene. Except to say 'yes sir' when I tell you to pick those flyers up and find somewhere to *put* them up!"

Something shifted inside Irene then. Something that had been coming for a long, long time.

These people were aliens from outer space.

Aliens who would rather let kids be broken and battered rather than admit they'd gotten it wrong about their cult leader.

Aliens who would never, ever believe Irene, their own daughter, over a toad like Brother Phillips.

"Fine," she said. "Let me go change, and I'll head out."

"Yes you will," her father said, satisfied.

Who needed to graduate high school, anyway?

Irene went upstairs. She'd change clothes, all right. But first...

She went to her parents' room. The old army foot-locker sat at the end of the bed, held shut by a combination lock.

With silent fingers, Irene spun the dial. 0-3-1-6. Her father's favorite Bible verse.

The lock popped open, and she quickly rummaged under the sheets and blankets until she found the shoebox.

Just over two grand. Wouldn't last forever, but should get her a good ways down the road, so long as Vicky didn't break down.

She'd always wanted to go to Atlanta. If she drove straight through, she'd be there in time for lunch. She'd call herself by her first name, and her Grandma's last name and do whatever she wanted.

Yvonne Rudabaugh. Free spirit and vagabond.

And as far as she knew, there were exactly zero farms in Atlanta.

DIRK KNIGHT
THE CASE OF THE TURPIN TURPITUDE
JASON A. ADAMS
Author of Dirk Knight: The Case of the Rustled Ranch

To everyone who solves the case.

Chapter 1

The city never sleeps.

From Roswell to Jonesboro, from Smyrna to Stone Mountain. Atlanta hums and roars twenty-five hours a day.

The city has seen its share of movie stars, moguls, and mobsters. Saints and sinners living, loving, and dying in the mosquito-filled swampy air of this global hub of humanity.

Most people in the ATL are decent folk who mind their manners and do their jobs.

But, as with any mixed barrel, sometimes a rotten apple gets down in the middle of things to cause a spreading blight of trouble.

That's when the good citizens of Atlanta call on—

Dirk Knight, Private Eye.

Chapter 2

Wednesday. October third. 6:37 pm.

Dirk's breath came in harsh, ragged gasps. Purple and red starbursts exploded like tulip popcorn across his vision as the pink flowers in the wallpaper ahead of him grew and shrank in a disturbing way.

His heart pounded like a crack-addled jackhammer with a bent shaft, pulsing in his neck and temples.

He felt it even in a tongue that tasted like an old copper penny, baked in the hellish depths of Death Valley.

Dirk could smell himself in the steamy haze that hung over the rowing machine, forcing itself up his nostrils with every pull.

He'd been trying to make it to an hour for the first time, but thirty-seven minutes would have to do. No reason why getting in shape should be fatal.

Shutting off the machine's workout computer, Dirk got to his feet, glad he'd installed a barre bar. He felt no pain. Yet. But his legs felt like rubber bands on muscle relaxers.

He wobbled across the garage-cum-gym, not even looking at the elliptical machine Barb loved. Just watching her work the arms and pedals gave him a bad case of hives. She loved it, though. And said she didn't see how he could last even five minutes practicing for slave-galley work on the rower.

To each their own.

Wiping his dripping head with an old dishrag that would never again touch dishes, Dirk wobbled his shaky way through the garagym's inside door, and into heaven.

Barb, the woman he'd fallen for as soon as she walked into his life with the first case of his PI career, stood at a massive, cherry-red gas range, shaking a cast-iron pan, sending up ambrosial aromas that beckoned to Dirk's stomach like a siren to a Greek sailor.

"Dinner in fifteen," she said without looking up, adding a pinch of something yellow to the contents of the pan. "Plenty of time for you to take a quickie shower. Which you need, I might add. Phew!"

Grinning sheepishly, Dirk headed for to do Barb's bidding, bumping hips with her along the way.

What with the rowing machine, and martial arts classes three times a week, Dirk's own hips had lost their padding over the past few months.

Well, some of their padding, anyway. But at least he'd had to buy new pants, because his old pants were too *big*, for a welcome change.

Barb was a professionally trained chef by day, Trixie the Receptionist for Dirk Knight, Private Eye by night. Dirk himself had once been Jerry Farnsworth, going from downsized IT guy to licensed private investigator of the background-check variety while he dreamed of being Dirk Knight, a hard-boiled, fedora-wearing private dick on the case. Righting wrongs, protecting damsels, chasing down doers of dastardly deeds.

His first case, the one which brought Barb into his life, had lasted a whole day and earned him nothing but a few bruises and the knowledge that recipes can't be copyrighted.

And Barb. His idea to market the look of her salad dressings instead of their taste had got her started.

His second case, in which he managed to have his client arrested for embezzlement and tax evasion, had got him back in touch with one of his best buds from his server maintenance days—a shaggy, Hawaiian-shirt wearing hacker named Mike Kowalski. Mike had been slumming around in his rolling Hack-O-Matic, an old moving van converted to one big Wi-Fi antenna and filled with better high-tech hardware than could be purchased from any retail company.

Probably from more than a few alphabet agencies.

With the reward money they'd received for sending his racist asshat neighbor to the T-Men cleaners, they'd been able to put a good down payment on a nice little house in East Atlanta, just a few miles from the old ballpark and handily close to a MARTA train station. Plus, Barb was now the proud owner of Barb's Dream Truck, her very own food wagon. Not much space inside, but what that woman could do with a narrow walkway and a couple of propane hotplates blew his mind.

And his diet plan. But that's what rowing machines were for, and he'd spend every last bit of sweat he had for her peanut-butter pie.

Chapter 3

AFTER A SHOWER and some excellent food (he didn't even want to try pronouncing the fancy French name, but Barb said it was tuna steaks with horseradish sauce), Dirk lounged contentedly on the sofa, pants unbuttoned and passing happy little belches like a beached aquarium bubbler.

Barb joined him, graciously not sitting in his lap until he'd digested a bit, and they'd just turned on an old Kurt Russell action flick, when a jarring *brrriiiing* split the peaceful evening like a giant's meat cleaver.

"*Oooo,*" Barb squealed, pushing Dirk down when he tried to get up. "Huh-*uh*, big boy. You know the rules!"

She ran to the bedroom they'd converted into his Dirk Knight, PI office, where the same shabby wooden desk and creaky old oak chair waited.

Where the five-pound hunk of black Bakelite rotary phone *braaaanged* away.

Barb plunked her butt on the corner of the desk,

crossing her legs demurely and winking at Dirk as she snatched up the heavy receiver and held it to her ear.

"Dirk Knight Detective Agency, Trixie speaking. How may I help you?"

Barb had a lovely contralto voice. Not too high, not too deep. When she spoke, she usually sounded like a cheerful salesgirl, which is what she'd been before she decided to take the cooking plunge.

Trixie's voice was deep. Throaty. Honey-covered sonic seduction filled with more promise than an entire presidential campaign. Both parties.

"Why, yes. I'll see if Mr. Knight is available for a call. He doesn't usually accept calls after hours, Mister… Oh, excuse me. *Major* Turpin. Hold, please."

She pulled out her phone, set it to playing some light jazz, and set both it and the receiver gently on the desk. She came to him, wrapped her arms around him, nibbled his earlobe, and whispered something he didn't hear over the torrential flood of hormones.

"What was that?"

This time, she bit his ear, and he tried to yelp softly enough that the person on the other end of the phone wouldn't hear.

"I *said*, this Major Turpin guy wants to hire you. He wouldn't tell me why, says he'll only talk to you. Go get 'em, tiger."

With a regret deeper than the Marianas Trench, Dirk extricated himself from Barb's embrace and went to the phone.

"Knight here. Start talking."

He hoped all his practice of a tough, gravely growl was paying off.

"Knight. Sir. This is Major Terry Turpin, Georgia Air National Guard."

"No thanks, I'm not interested in enlisting."

"What? No…that is, I'm not calling on Guard business, Mr. Knight. This is rather a more personal—and delicate—situation."

Whipping out his spiral-bound pocket notebook, Dirk flipped it open. Realized he didn't have a pen. Tried to get around the desk without tangling himself or anything else in the handset's cord. No wonder most all phones had gone cordless.

Barb saved him, passing him a cheap ball-point with *Barb's Dream Truck* stamped on the barrel.

"Thanks, doll," he said, then scratched at a blank page on the notebook until the ink started flowing.

"Shoot, Major. What's the dope?"

"Dope? I assure you, Mr. Knight. No drugs are involved."

Geez. Did no one read the classics anymore? Dirk sighed and massaged his forehead.

"What's the job, Turpin?"

"Ah. Yes. Well…"

There was that Army Intelligence everyone raved about.

Turpin cleared his throat and tried again.

"It's about my wife, Mr. Knight. You see, I'm part of the full-time cadre at the base. Not just a weekender. And…I think…well, that is to say, I believe a certain lieutenant in my command…is maybe visiting my house when I'm on duty."

"Uh-huh. So you think your wife is getting busy with the underlings in between drill weekends?"

More throat clearing.

"I don't know for sure, you understand. But I *have* to know. And I've not been able to catch the dirty…ah, catch them in the act. Could you maybe, I don't know, follow them? Do a stakeout at my place?"

"Address?" Dirk wrote *Turpin Turpitude* across the top. He wasn't sure if that was the right word, but it had a nice ring to it. And a stakeout? That would be cool as hell.

The major rattled off a street name and number up in Smyrna. Not to far from the Guard's airfield.

"I'll get started first thing tomorrow, Major Turpin. My standard fee for this sort of work is…" He looked over at Barb, who held up three fingers with a smile and a wink. "Three hundred up front, then another three a day. Plus expenses. Trixie will take your payment information." She already had her cash register app open on her phone, finger poised.

A quick gasp. Another clearing of a majorly throat.

"That seems…ah…reasonable. And about how long will it take, do you think?"

"That depends. How often would you say your wife hooks up with this Looey?"

He handed the phone to Barb so she could begin harvesting a chunk of soldier cash.

Chapter 4

THE NEXT MORNING found Dirk driving slowly along a tree-lined street crowded on both sides with postwar ranch house blandness dressed in white picket fencing. His baby blue Corolla didn't really fit in with the suburban assault vehicles in some of the driveways, but he doubted he'd draw much attention.

If he had a vintage Chevy Fleetmaster or Styleline, now. One of these days.

321...323...325...

He scanned each house number, thankfully attached to garage or front doors in sturdy, six-inch-high black steel. Gotta love the new 911 requirements.

Ah, there it was. 333 Fernberry Lane. Only half evil.

The major's butt-parking pad looked like most of the other houses on the street. One floor. Drab, tar-and-gravel roof tiles sloping down to eaves not nearly deep enough to catch the breeze. Red brick. Yard flat and grassed. Cut so short it might as well be artificial turf. Low red-berried hedges trimmed to a military flattop below a bay window that let him see into a white-walled, white-carpeted living room.

With a white sofa? Geez. The major's moll might be inviting people over just to see different colors.

He parked down the street and killed the engine. Angled the rearview mirror so he could see the major's front door and garage. Tried to calm the thrill in his belly.

Dirk Knight on the stakeout. A cool character ready to turn hot in an instant when his client's nemesis appeared. Ready to risk life and limb in pursuit of his goal...

Ready to eat the upholstery, after two hours of staring at nothing. Stakeouts in the movies were never this *boring*.

Then he had an idea. A way to get more information on the easy. And a way to have some company. He picked up his Bluetooth handset, a modified copy of the handset on his antique phone back at the office, and called the guy who'd cobbled it together for him.

"Yo, Jerry! I mean, Dirk, m'man. What's shakin,' dude?"

"Hey, Mike. You busy? Want to have some fun? Maybe make a few bucks?"

"Sure. As long as you don't make me do a W-9 or any of that bogus government shit."

Dirk laughed. Same old Mike.

"No sweat, dude. Come up to Smyrna, to Fernberry Lane. Look for my car. I'll even chip in on gas for your cyberbeast."

"Oh, shit baby. I'm all about that. Gimme forty-five and I'm there."

Chapter 5

FORTY-FIVE TURNED out to be sixty-eight, but Dirk finally got his eyelids open when he heard the badly-in-need-of-exhaust-work blat of Mike's hackerwagon.

Mike's uncle owned a couple of Y'all Haul franchises, and had given his favorite miscreant nephew one of the older trucks, providing both housing and lab space for one of the city's best hacker not behind bars.

Of course, the fact that he'd never been arrested might make him the city's *best* hacker.

Dirk, in his Jerry Farnsworth days, hadn't been into that side of things. He'd been a mechanic. The guy who built servers and workstations, and who fixed them when they pooped the bed.

Mike, on the other hand…

He'd started at the same company Dirk worked for, first as a code monkey, then as project lead for a new internet crawler. Mike hadn't been thrilled about helping "The Man" snoop on people's browsing habits or personal websites, and had ended up modifying the bot program to harvest everything public concerning the company's board of directors.

Public, and a few things not so public.

Dirk wasn't sure how Mike's final conversation with the poohbahs went, but he ended up laid off, not fired and incarcerated.

Must've been some good stuff in the bot's vacuum bag.

"So what's the scoop, man?" Mike asked as Dirk hauled himself up into the van's high-tech cargo area, taking a moment to appreciate all the blinky high tech lights.

Dirk explained the particulars of the case.

"Can you hack into the major's WI-FI network? And then snoop any running computers?"

Mike snorted.

"Can a capitalist love money? Gimme a sec."

He plopped into his rolling stool and began finger-dancing his way along several keyboards, watching as the van's three monitors filled with the kind of programmer gobbledygook that always gave Dirk a headache.

An archaic chime that reminded Dirk of an ancient Macintosh's startup tone filled the bay.

"In like Flynn, m'man. People never bother changing their router's default admin creds." He laced his fingers together and cracked his knuckles. "Two shakes while I see what all wifey left up and running."

More rattling keys. Muttering from Mike as he stared at the screens. Then...

"Bingo, boyo. Got one live laptop. The DVR's on, but not the smart idiot box. Let's see... Okay. Standard Microshaft laptop. Winblows 10. No protection. Well, not *good* protection. I'm in."

Dirk put a hand on Mike's shoulder and leaned in to stare at the monitor, like he knew what he was looking at.

"Can you get a remote desktop session?"

Another snort as what was presumably the Turpin desktop flashed onto the second monitor.

He and Mike poked and prodded through the laptop. Checking the email account, looking through the files, playing a quick game of solitaire each.

And not finding anything useful.

"Rats," Dirk said, slapping the workbench. "I was hoping to get something before… Hang on."

He'd heard a car going by, then slowing.

A quick check through a crack under the van's sliding rear door confirmed his suspicion.

A car had just turned into the Turpins' driveway. And not the major's little red Corvette.

"You got any exterior views in this thing?" he asked Mike.

"You got it, m'man."

The left-hand monitor switched to a hi-res view of the street behind the van. Dirk watched as a man got out of a dark green Taurus and went to the door.

He didn't knock, but the door opened anyway, revealing a slim, athletic woman wearing slim, athletic stretchpants and a damp tanktop.

"Uh-oh. Lieutenant Willie's about to penetrate the—"

"Yeah, yeah," Dirk said. "Keep your mind out of the gutter, would you? Damn. I wish I'd remembered my sonic ear."

"That box store contraption?" Mike said, bushy eyebrows raised. "You gotta get on the ball if you're gonna be a good dick, dick."

He wheeled a pole on wheels over to the door. The pole held a metal bowl that looked big enough to whip up a salad for a ball park. From the center jutted a good facsimile of Larry King's broadcast microphone.

"Just let me get 'er jacked in, and…"

"*—told you I own you, get me?*"

"*I can't, Tom. I just can't!*"

"*You will, baby. You'll do it or I'll—*"

The sound of flesh striking flesh. A woman screamed, then began sobbing.

"*Okay, okay! I'll do it. I'll do it all, Tom. Please don't—*"

Dirk didn't hear the rest. He had the van's door rolled up and was pounding down the sidewalk toward the Turpin house.

Chapter 6

BY THE TIME Dirk reached the front door, sweat rolled down his face. But he wasn't too winded to his surprise and delight. The rowing machine was paying off!

He studied the door, wondering if a good karate kick would be enough to break it open.

Then he heard the shots.

A barrage of gunfire. All coming from inside the house.

"Give it up, Flanagan! We've got you surrounded!"

"Come and get me, copper! You'll never take me alive!"

More shots rang out as Dirk emerged from the shrub he'd jumped behind. Good thing Barb wasn't here to see her Brave Detective Man nearly wet himself over *The Johnstone Affair*.

He should have recognized the dialog right away. He'd seen the 1957 noir classic a dozen times. The TV must really be cranked.

Well, he was here now. Might as well do his best.

Dirk pushed the glowing button beside the door,

hoping Mrs. Turpin or her visitor would hear it over the final scene.

"Jerry! I mean, hey Dirk!" Mike yelled, hustling down the sidewalk and waving his arm. "Hang on a sec, man! Don't—"

But just then the door opened.

"Yes? Can I help you?" Mrs. Turpin asked. She still wore the sweaty workout clothes.

She was still sweating, but her puffy red eyes, damp cheeks, and runny nose didn't say exercise.

Behind her, Jerry could see her visitor sitting on the white couch, file folders spread across the coffee table.

"Um, sorry to trouble you, ma'am. My name is Dirk Knight. I'm a private investigator." After a couple of tries, he got his ID wallet free of his breast pocket and flashed his license. "Your husband hired me to—"

"Come in, Mr. Farnsworth," said the guy at the couch. He stood, stretched, and walked toward them, hand out. "Let him in, Mrs. Turpin. Might as well get the air cleared."

"Don't do it, m'man!" Mike said, panting up to the door and holding his side. "It's *the* man! The feds!"

"Michael Kowalski. It's truly an honor, sir," the fed said, switching his offered hand to the shaggy-haired hacker. "I studied your work in a seminar last year. Your information-gathering protocols revolutionized our data search and gather capabilities."

"I...what? Really? You've seen my code?" Mike's cheeks were turning as red as a little Corvette.

"Absolutely. And we at the agency love your stuff. Come in, Mr. Kowalski. And you too, Mr. Farnsworth."

"It's Knight," Dirk said. "I had my name legally changed last—"

"Last November. Yes. Forgive me."

They followed the guy in the suit and the gal in the stretchpants into the living room. Dirk sat in a leatherette recliner (white), while Mike sat cross-legged on the carpet.

"I'm Special Agent Wilbur Hopkins," he said, flashing his own ID and badge. "US Treasury Department. Mrs. Turpin here was just trying to explain a few curious deposits into the family bank account. Deposits that just so happen to match amounts withdrawn from the general expense account at her husband's base."

"I was trying to tell you, man," Mike said, poking Dirk's shin. "The Man's been all over your boy Turpin's computer. Cell phone, too. I think they even got a tracker on his car, but I didn't have time to pin that down."

Agent Hopkins whistled, impressed.

"Have you considered a career with the United States government?" he said. "We could offer you—"

"No way, tax man," Mike said, shaking his head like a tambourine. "I ain't working for The Man. Besides, I already got a job with the Dirk Knight Detective Agency."

Dirk figured he'd better say…something.

"So you two haven't been…ah…"

"No!" Mrs. Turpin said hotly. As hotly as a sniveling person can, anyway. "I couldn't believe what Agent Hopkins told me when he first came around, two weeks ago. I thought he was just a junior officer in Terry's unit. But he's been *spying* on us!"

"I've been conducting a special investigation at the behest of both the Georgia Air National Guard, and the Treasury Department," Hopkins said patiently. "Embezzlement would usually be handled by the Georgia authorities, but in this case the military has jurisdiction over the crimes at the base, since Major Turpin is a regular officer on the full-time staff. And us T-men—and I haven't heard that one in years, by the way—have jurisdiction over the tax evasion." He sighed dramatically and looked heavenward. "These people always seem to forget to claim the extra income on their 1040."

"I just can't believe it," Mrs. Turpin said, sinking down onto the couch and sobbing into a tissue. "Terry's going to go to prison. And I might, too!"

"Now, now, Mrs. Turpin," Hopkins said as he began gathering up his folders. "We'll check it out, of course, but if you had no knowledge of your husband's actions, there's no need for you to worry about jail time."

Mike poked Dirk's shin again, then he stood up.

"Hey, Dirk? Got a sec, m'man?" He jerked his head toward the door, subtle as a chainsaw.

Dirk followed Mike outside.

"What's up, dude?"

"I was playing around with the neighborhood cell network before all that business with the movie and you running off like an idiot."

Dirk let it slide. He *had* been an idiot.

"So?"

"So there are three active cell phone signals in that house," Mike said. "You'd figure there would be two, right? The Man's and the lady's. So what's the third one all about? I didn't see any pictures of kids or anything."

"Huh. Interesting. Any idea where to look in a three-thousand-square-foot house for a six-inch rectangle?"

"Not yet," Mike said with a grin. "But gimme a sec."

He pulled a small plastic box from his pocket. It looked like a pocket voltmeter, with a needle that could sweep along a numbered semicircle of lines. But this voltmeter had two antennas.

Mike tugged on each rabbit ear until they were about a foot long, thumbed a switch on the side of the gadget, and headed back inside.

Dirk followed, wondering what he was up to.

"Mr. Kowalski?" Hopkins said, staring at the contraption in Mike's hand. "What—"

Dirk held up a hand as he followed Mike down the hall.

"Agent Hopkins? Do you have a valid search warrant for the premises? One which includes all electronic devices?"

"Of course," Hopkins said. "But I already have the laptop and Mrs. Turpin's phone."

"That's right," she said in a shrill voice. "That's all there is, I swear."

"Didn't your mama teach you that swearing ain't ladylike?" Mike said, staring at his magic box's dancing needle as he entered a bedroom with (of course) a white dresser and a queen-sized bed covered with a white quilt.

"Hey Dirk, m'man. Mind lifting up the mattress?"

Dirk's curiosity was definitely up now.

He picked up a corner of the mattress, revealing a cell phone. One of the cheap, prepaid kind. What some folks called a burner. Not attached to anyone's name, no service plan to link it to an individual.

"Hey, Agent Hopkins," Dirk called. "Might want to check this out. But better put on a pair of gloves, first."

"That's not mine!" Mrs. Turpin squealed from the living room. "I've never seen that before!"

A minute later, Hopkins came into the bedroom, one latex-gloved hand clamped around Mrs. Turpin's arm. He looked down at the phone, and shook his head sadly.

"Mrs. Turpin, what are the chances I won't find any illicit banking software on yon tiny phone? Or any of your fingerprints?"

Chapter 7

Two days later, Dirk and Mike were manfully working their way through the huge spread of gustatory goodies Barb had cooked up to celebrate their success.

"Fraud, embezzlement, and tax evasion," Dirk said around a mouthful of Barb's exquisite peanut butter pie. "Pretty much the same slew of charges that Mrs. Marshall got last July, except this time there's a bunch of military stuff thrown in."

"Oh, Dirk honey. I'm so proud of you for cracking the case!"

Barb hugged his neck and planted a big, wet smooch on his lips. When she drew back, Dirk saw he'd managed to transfer some peanut butter pie to his sweetie.

"Hey, never would have happened without Mike's magic box," he said modestly.

"Yes, but *you* brought Mike in on the case, honey. And *you* are the Private Eye, my dashing hero-man."

"No shit, m'man," Mike said, scraping up the last of

his own slice of pie. Dirk didn't usually share, but payback is only fair. "You can keep all the credit. I don't want any of those fed guys knowing any more about me than they already do. Feel free to go halfsies with the reward dough, though."

It was Dirk's turn to snort.

"Says the dude that just picked up a gig writing training manuals for the Treasury Department Cyber Investigations office."

Mike blushed and reached for the pie pan. What the hell. He deserved seconds.

"What can I say? The Man knows quality."

"Since you're working for the government now, I got you a little something," Barb said, handing a small box to Mike. "Wear it in good health, to every meeting with your new contractees."

Mike groaned when he opened the box and pulled out a purple necktie covered with tiny white writing.

"A *tie?* Why not just put my head in a hangman's noose?"

"Read it," she said, a mischievous glint in her eyes.

Mike squinted at the miniscule lettering, then he busted out a huge guffaw, spraying crumbs of pie crust across the table.

"What does it say?" Dirk asked as Barb giggled.

Mike threw the tie at him, laughing too hard to answer.

In short order, Dirk had joined his honey and his best pal, laughing as he read the same words, repeated at least a thousand time.

Fuck The Man!

JASON A. ADAMS

Beauty

For those who rescue us.

Chapter 1

DANNY ELKINS ENJOYED the single life.

A thirty year old confirmed bachelor, he'd been able to land a good-paying job at one of the biggest airlines in town, keeping their email servers humming and collecting enough every two weeks that he'd been able to buy an old, un-remodeled bungalow in an old, un-gentrified neighborhood.

The ancient cedar siding on the outside, the holly bushes and mulberry trees somewhere between unpruned and feral outside, and the beautiful old coal-grate fireplaces, bone-colored subway tile, and original lath-and-plaster walls inside charmed the shit out of him. Quite the change, coming home from a noisy, overlit and overchilled data center to this little slice of the jazz age.

Amber light from the setting sun filled his tiny kitchen, painting the walls the color of good orange blossom honey while he whipped up his favorite Saturday night meal. "Whatever's in the fridge" stir-fry.

This evening, that meant a little bit of jasmine rice left over from takeout two days ago. A few bits of celery and green onion that still had enough stiff in their bristles for some crunch. A couple of eggs and some tofu for protein.

And his special blend of good, peppery olive oil and some nice, toasty sesame oil.

Not even half done, and the kitchen smelled like heaven.

Ian Anderson sang about solstice bells from the Bluetooth speakers paired to his phone, and Danny added his own voice. He'd never sing where anyone else could hear him, but in his own kitchen?

Let the crockery rock, the windows rattle, and his dulcet tones roll.

He dished up his din-din in an empty margarine tub. He wasn't looking to impress anyone, and the last bits of buttery residue would add a bit more flavor.

Plus, he could throw away the dishes instead of washing them. Bonus.

Flopping down on the couch, he grabbed the remote to see what bad old movies he could find for his solo dinner theater.

And paused.

He could swear he'd heard…

There it was again.

A high-pitched, keening wail.

Not human, and Danny was pretty sure he didn't believe in banshees.

Whatever or whoever it was cried out again.

Call 911? Turn the music back on? Earplugs, maybe?

But something in that cry poked him in the blood pump.

Animal or human, that wasn't a grown thing's voice.

Shit.

Danny set the stir-fry tub on the characterless IKEA coffee table, tied the drawstring on his stained gray sweatpants (making sure to tie them high enough that his belly didn't pooch out under his t-shirt), and went out onto the front porch, shivering as the damp coolness reminded him he should have grabbed his flannel.

And there it was again. Coming from next door.

Sounded like…a puppy, maybe? Not a high-pitched *yike* of pain.

No, this was the long, drawn-out shrill crying of hopeless despair.

That might be a little melodramatic, but it felt right.

Argh.

Danny didn't need this hassle. He had a new rack of servers arriving Monday morning, and would be spending most of the week on installation and configuration. He needed his weekend, dammit!

The cry rang out again.

Okay, fine. He'd find whatever it was, take it to a shelter, and get back to his peace and quiet.

Chapter 2

Rooowoo-woo

Definitely not a grown…whatever. And definitely coming from under the Rose of Sharon bushes alongside the house beside Danny's.

That house had been empty for close to a year. He missed J.D., the old coot who'd lived there until he passed at the tender young age of eighty-seven.

He'd never met J.D.'s kids, but the house was the center of an all-out probate war, from what he'd heard.

And now was the site of drama and distress of some sort.

Grateful for the tiny LED penlight he kept on his keyring, Danny crouched down and began duck-walking along the row of bushes, listening for another keen and sweeping the light back and forth.

At first, he thought it was just a sand-colored rock. Or maybe a good-sized Yukon Gold potato.

But neither potatoes nor rocks shy away when you reach for them.

Still not sure what he'd found, although the fur

ruled out reptile or fish, Danny put the light back in his pocket before cradling the shivering lump in his hands and carefully picking it up.

She, not *it*.

In his hands, dwarfed in spite of the fact Danny ran to the small side, lay a tiny girl pup.

Jesus, she couldn't be ready to leave her mama. She still had the puppy pot belly, and her wide, skittish eyes were newborn blue.

"Shhhh… It's gonna be okay, girl."

Maybe.

Danny didn't kid himself. He knew bupkes about animals. Never had a cat or dog, or even a goldfish growing up. His dad had been the type who believed the perfect animal came medium-rare and smothered in gravy.

He felt something warm and damp against his index finger as he carried his bundle back to his own porch.

He stopped directly under the porch light to get a better look at the urchin. The dampness he felt was her tiny tongue, licking his finger.

Angry-looking and scaly raised red circles pushed through the puppy fuzz covering her little round body. That couldn't be good.

Shit. Didn't he pass a vet clinic between here and work every day? He might ought to take her in, make sure she wasn't sick or anything.

Then he'd take her to the shelter.

Tucking the pup in the crook of his elbow, Danny went back in to fetch keys and wallet. And his flannel shirt.

And to put his dinner in the fridge. Maybe he could microwave it later without melting the butter tub.

Pup Girl barely stirred the whole time, except to burrow deeper against him.

"Don't get comfortable," he muttered, feeling foolish. "I'm a solo act, get it?"

There was that tongue again, licking the inside of his arm.

It got worse on the way to the vet, of course.

He'd put her in the passenger seat of his car, over which he'd laid his oldest towel to keep things tidy and stain-free. And what did the little ingrate do as soon as they were on the road and he couldn't stop her?

She'd wriggled her way across the console and into his lap, where she curled up and promptly began snoring in cute little whistles, like a cartoon teakettle.

He only scratched her head at the red lights.

Chapter 3

Fortunately for Danny, and for his waif, Stonega
Veterinary Hospital was not only where he remembered it, but also open for walk-ins until nine every
night.

The damp had turned to drizzle during the trip,
and he tucked the girl inside his flannel before opening
the door and heading inside. He'd never been in a vet's
office, but it didn't look much different than any other
clinic, at least not up front. Shiny white linoleum floor,
long counter with signs for check in and check out,
posters all about good health all over the walls.

And lining shelves in an attached open area, a
plethora of stuffed toys, miniature feline fishing poles,
rubber balls, leashes, and all the other assorted animal
accoutrements.

A young kid whose nametag announced him as
Braiden welcomed them in, "aww"-ed at the sight of
the sandy, four-footed potato, and paged the on-duty
vet while Danny sat himself and Pup Girl in an uncom-

fortable plastic chair designed to discourage lengthy waiting.

Luckily, the wait wasn't long. He and she were the only two in the lobby, and before five minutes went by, out came a perky brunette in green scrubs and white jacket, her long hair in a ponytail. Probably a tech who'd take all the pup's vitals, prep everything, and abscond with Danny's credit card information.

"Hello, Mr. Elkins," she said, offering her hand. "I'm Dr. Sizemore. Is this our little bundle of joy?"

She reached down to scratch Pup Girl's ears and look at her scaly hide. The pup gave a tiny whine, but didn't pull away.

Danny, a little taken aback at this child with credentials, shook her hand.

"Yep. Found her under a cabbage leaf."

She raised an eyebrow, one of those tricks he'd never mastered himself, and he clarified.

"Okay, under a bush at the empty house next door. No sign of mama, no collar, no nothing. I think she has mange or something, but I really don't know anything about dogs."

"Hmm… Let's take her back and have a gander. C'mon, exam room four, second on the right."

Pup Girl firmly in hand, he followed Dr. Sizemore back to a small cubbyhole of a room. What with the cabinets and shelving along the far wall, and a waist-high stainless-steel table taking up half the space, there was barely room enough for one computer geek, one vet, and one potato.

"Just set her on the table, please," Dr. Sizemore said, opening a drawer and pulling out a pair of blue exam gloves and a thermometer.

Danny and Pup Girl both winced as Dr. Sizemore

took her temperature, but thankfully it was over quickly.

"A little elevated, but not too bad, considering all the ringworm." She went back to the cabinets and began shuffling through the contents.

"Ringworm?" Danny had heard of it, but wasn't sure what all it meant. "Is that bad?"

Holding a trigger pump spray bottle, the doc turned back to him, face somber.

"I don't know how to tell you this, Mr. Elkins, but she's going to be just fine."

Danny blinked, opened his mouth to say…something, then she burst out laughing.

"I'm sorry, that was terrible. But I couldn't resist. Your face…" She laughed again.

Danny could feel the heat in his face, but for some reason, he didn't mind. She had a great laugh, and she had definitely zinged him a good one.

On the table, Pup Girl made a "Mrrp" sound and tried to run for it, but her tiny feet couldn't get any purchase on the shiny metal.

"Oh no you don't," Dr. Sizemore said, bringing her free hand down like the pay gate at a parking garage. "Not until we get you hosed down."

She liberally spritzed the wriggling, protesting Pup Girl until both she and the table were soaked.

"It's a simple anti-fungal spray," she said, setting the bottle aside before massaging Pup Girl gently. "This will kill whatever's close to the skin surface, and I'll send her home with a week's worth of pills to be given morning and evening. That should have everything cleared up in no time, but it'll take a bit for the fur to re-grow in the lesions."

Danny nodded along like he knew what she was

talking about. The only thing he knew about fungal anything was the athlete's foot he battled every summer.

The vet took a ratty-looking pink towel from a bin full of similarly despondent bath linens and wrapped Pup Girl up like a burrito.

Pup Girl "Mrrp"-ed again, and licked her finger.

"Yes, you're right, good girl. It *is* awfully cozy, isn't it?"

Dr. Sizemore spent the next few minutes shining lights into openings, checking barely-there needle teeth, and being generally veterinarianish.

Danny stood out of the way, hands in his pockets. He wasn't worried about this foundling puppy.

Not when he meant to take her to a shelter anyway.

Next week.

After the pills were done.

"How is she?" he asked when Dr. Sizemore finally stopped puttering.

Dr. Sizemore took a miniature tablet from the pocket of her white coat and began tapping away.

"Well, not too shabby, considering. She's *very* young. Probably four or five weeks. A little malnourished from the looks of things, but I don't think we need bloodwork just yet. Mainly what she needs is to kick the ringworm, and to spend some time somewhere safe, warm, and dry. I'll get you some high nutrition puppy food, and get Beauty here that medication."

The urchin, who'd been blinking and drooping like any kid up past her bedtime, perked up when Dr. Sizemore said "Beauty," her ears coming up and forward, one standing and one flopping.

Dr. Sizemore gave that fantastic laugh again and rubbed her tiny head.

"Beauty? Is that your name, good girl?"

"Mrrp."

Beauty. Why not? He couldn't keep calling her potato or Pup Girl.

He scooped up the be-toweled Beauty and followed Dr. Sizemore back out front, where she handed him a shopping basket and began filling it with the necessities.

"Puppy kibble," she said, dropping a rattling sack in the basket. "No wet food until she's older, but you can soften this stuff with a little milk if she has trouble cracking it down." Next, she grabbed what looked like a pack of diapers off another shelf.

"Training pads. Also known as piddle pads. You'll want to make sure she's never far from one until she's old enough for housebreaking. Which reminds me…" She snatched a round plastic bottle with a cartoonish dog looking guilty on the label. "Stain remover. Gotta have that."

Next came a small plastic pet carrier, and a small bag of miniature dog biscuits.

"She can have a quarter biscuit after pill time, to help make sure she keeps the medicine down. I think that's everything you'll need, Mr. Elkins."

"It's just Danny, Dr. Sizemore," he said, distracted by something on the shelf nearest the checkout counter. "Mr. Elkins makes me feel like a math teacher."

On impulse, he picked up a fuzzy purple plush toy, either a dinosaur or a cow, he couldn't quite tell.

"Do you think this would be good? I know it's almost as big as she is, but…"

He saw that she was staring at him, the corners of her lips sneaking upward.

"I think that's a fine choice, Danny. Now let's get you two headed home so Beauty here can get some sleep. Make sure you pick up some athlete's foot spray on the way. If you feel any itches on yourself, give 'em a spritz. Don't want you to break out in rosy donuts."

Chapter 4

THE NEXT MORNING, Danny was terrified.

The night hadn't gone exactly smoothly, but he'd managed to stop Beauty's mewling by putting her on the bed. She hadn't made a mess, either, so that was good.

But this morning, she didn't want to get up. She just laid there on the mattress beside her half-empty food bowl, making that *mrrp* noise.

He'd barely been able to get her to swallow the pill, or to eat the half-biscuit to chase it down.

Hunting through the pocket of his sweatpants, he found the folded-up receipt from the vet's office, wincing as he remembered the smell of burning credit card.

Braiden obviously worked evenings, since the chipper young lady who answered said her name was Jayda.

"I'm sorry, Mr. Elkins. Dr. Sizemore is off today. Let's see here…" Computer keys clacked. "I see a note to page her if you called about Miss Beauty. Can I have a number where she can reach you?"

Danny sighed in relief, and quickly gave his cell number. He didn't care how much Dr. Sizemore billed him, he was just glad she was on call or whatever.

He was trying to interest Beauty in a piece of bacon when his phone rang.

"Hello?"

"Danny, hi. It's Ellen Sizemore from last night. Jayda says Beauty took a turn for the worse last night?"

"Yeah," he said, looking over at his girl, who had rolled onto her back, pudgy legs stuck out all over. "She doesn't seem interested in anything, and I can't get her to move around or eat or drink or anything."

Bless her, Dr. Sizemore put on the calm, cool, and collected voice Danny himself used when management freaked out over some IT fiasco.

"You're on Sycamore Street, right? In Maple Heights? I'm only a couple of miles away. Sit tight, Danny. Keep Beauty calm. I'm on my way."

And she was. Less than fifteen minutes later, he heard a car pull in the driveway, and then a door slam.

He ran to the front door, hitching up his pajama bottoms and pulling the door open before she could knock.

"Thank you so, so much for coming, Dr. Sizemore. Beauty's in the bedroom."

He left the door standing open and rushed back to his bed, where Beauty had started up with the teakettle snores again.

Behind him, Dr. Sizemore stifled a cough.

"And how long did you say she's been like this?"

He turned to see her lips twitching again.

"Well, I don't know, Dr. Sizemore. I woke up and

saw her that way, and that she hadn't finished her food from last night."

He noticed for the first time that Dr. Sizemore wasn't in her Dr. outfit this morning. Instead, she wore black stretchpants and a faded Michigan State t-shirt the color of a nauseated leprechaun.

Not that *he* cared how good she looked in street clothes.

"So can you tell what's wrong with her?"

"I can, and I'll even tell you if you promise to call me Ellen, *Danny*."

From the bed came a sound a lot like a mouse-sized belch.

"Okay, Ellen. What's wrong with my dog?"

She picked up the kibble bag she'd sent him home with, hefting it in her hand and squeezing down from the top to where the kibble finally started.

"Exactly how much food was in her bowl when you went to bed?"

Danny shuffled his feet. Felt the heat in his face again.

"Well, she was still hungry after—"

"*How* much?"

He wished he'd put on real pants with pockets. He didn't have anywhere for his hands.

"I guess maybe she had two whole bowls and what's left now. I mean, what isn't left."

"I see." Ellen dropped the bag and pointed at the bed.

"*Sit*, mister. Stay. After you put a training pad under Beauty, she's going to need it."

Ellen left the bedroom and headed toward…his kitchen?

Danny got a piddle pad under Beauty as she *mrrp-*

ed sleepily. From the kitchen, he heard drawers opening and closing.

Finally Ellen came back to the bedroom, brandishing a metal eighth-cup measure at him.

"*One* scoop in the morning, okay? Then *one* more when you get home from work. And *one* more before bedtime. And that's *all*, got it?"

Danny gave his bare feet a good looking over. He hadn't felt like this since his mom caught him sneaking a peek at his dad's girlie magazines when he was thirteen.

"She seemed hungry, is all," he said. Or muttered.

"Rule one of children from all species. Kids lie relentlessly when it comes to their stomachs."

From the piddle pad came the sound of air squeaking out a pinched balloon.

Ellen laughed that laugh again, and Danny felt more heat. In his face, and in his chest this time.

"She'll be fine, Danny. I don't envy you the cleanup later, but she's not sick. Just stuffed to the gills."

Danny fumbled with the useless hands in his lap.

"Thanks, Doc. Ellen. I'm sorry you had to come all the way here just to tell me I'm an idiot. What do I owe you?"

Beauty snorted, rolled back onto her belly, and crawled on top of her fuzzy purple cowasaur before promptly putting the teakettle back to the boil.

"For the hero who rescued Beauty from certain death?" she said. "And I'm serious about that. As cold and rainy as it was last night, she wouldn't have made it." She smiled and tilted her head to one side. "I think the proper fee would be breakfast. Bagels okay? There's a great place over on Hawthorne that delivers."

As it turned out, Beauty, bagels, and bad old movies on a Sunday morning were a fine way to start. Especially when sitting with good company who knew all about dogs.

Danny enjoyed the single life, but maybe he'd found something better.

He never did get around to calling the animal shelter.

ABOUT JASON

Jason A. Adams writes across the spectrum. His stories include science fiction, fantasy, horror, Appalachian folk tales, and sometimes a little romance here and there.

You can find more of his work and sign up for updates from his Brain Squirrels at www.jason-adams.info, and in the pages of *Pulphouse Magazine*, most recently in issue #10. His stories have also appeared in the 2019 and 2020 Winter Holiday Spectaculars from WMG Publishing. Several more stories will appear in upcoming issues of *Pulphouse Magazine* and Holiday Spectaculars, so stay tuned!

Jason, a recovering Air Force brat who grew up all over the US and Japan, now perches in the mountains of Southwest Virginia with his beautiful wife Kari Kilgore, four spoiled cats, and assorted wild visitors from the nearby forest.

news@jasonadams.info

facebook.com/Jason.A.Adams.2

ALSO BY JASON A. ADAMS

I hope you enjoyed reading the stories in *Capeless Heroes* as much as I enjoyed writing them.

Visit www.jasonadams.info and join the adventure for exclusive new fiction, my past and future travels, and whatever else strikes my fancy. Hope to see you there!

Novellas:

Agonist

Short Stories:

Mick of Malvern: Seeker for Hire (A Hard-Boiled Fairy Tale)

To Catch a Thief (An Appalachian Gothic Tale)

Sunlit Dispositions (A Hard-Boiled Space Opera)

GS-304

Angel of Mercy

Cupids

The Green Knight

Oppositional

Birth of the Makmorn

Collections and Anthologies:

Near Future Forward (with Kari Kilgore)

Partners in Romance (with Kari Kilgore)

Tales From the Squirrel Garden: Volume 1

Through the Squirrel Tree

ADDITIONAL COPYRIGHT INFORMATION

Dirk Knight: The Case of the Turpin Turpitude

Beauty